# CALYX

## of Jeversal

# CALYX

## of Teversall

## MAIA APPLEBY

Illustrations by Angela Souza

AN IMPRINT OF BRIGHTER BOOKS PUBLISHING HOUSE

Platypus, an Imprint of Brighter Books Publishing House
Visit our website at: www.brighterbooks.com

First Published: December 2011

ISBN 978-1-927004-02-9 - Trade Paperback Edition

Library and Archives Canada Cataloguing in Publication

Appleby, Maia, 1970-
Calyx of Teversall / written by Maia Appleby ; illustrated by Angela Souza.

Also issued in electronic format.
ISBN 978-1-927004-02-9 (pbk.).--ISBN 978-1-927004-03-6 (bound)

I. Souza, Angela  II. Title.

PZ7.A643Ca 2011            j813'.6            C2011-905332-2

Illustrations © 2011 Angela Souza

*In memory of Kelly Berthelot -- an amazing young woman who put her heart into everything she did. We will miss your funny spirit and kindness, and hope the horses in heaven have wings.*

Printed and bound in the USA on acid-free paper that contains no material from old-growth forests, using ink that is safe for children. One tree has been planted for this book.

For Taryn & Cody

# Chapters

# Chapter 1

The Blythe family had all the necessities. They had a small farm with fertile soil, a few hens, a vegetable garden, some fruit trees, and—most importantly—two good grain fields that they alternated to ensure a bountiful wheat harvest each year. Their modest stone cottage was strong, comforting, and neatly whitewashed with a snugly thatched roof, a wood cook stove, and a separate fireplace. In the four years since the couple had moved to Rimmolan, purchasing their property with what little they had saved, they had attained this.

Charles knew everything about wheat. He knew when to sow it, how to harvest it, how many seeds to save, how to keep the soil productive, how to separate the grain, and how to use the straw. He even thatched the roof himself.

Sigrid spent much of her time in the workroom at the back of the cottage, turning the unruly dried blades of straw into neatly plaited bundles that could be used by others to make bonnets, mats, or countless other useful objects. The straw was like gold to them, although unlike the fabled miller's daughter, rather than spin, she braided.

She was twenty years old when Charlie was born. The child had his mother's light hair, his father's deep blue eyes, and the natural ingenuity of both of them combined. He learned to plait straw when he was just three years old. Sometimes, his mother would spend an entire day halving the long stems with the sharpened bone blade of the wanzer, her prized straw-splitting tool, while the toddler sat on the floor braiding and braiding an endless rope of flattened wheat stalks until the strand seemed long enough to be rolled into a bundle for Sigrid to sell.

She liked his company. In rural Rimmolan, some of the straw plaiters visited one another and talked while doing their work, but it was inconvenient to haul all the supplies around when neighbors lived so far apart. Charles Senior was out doing chores throughout most of the day. Little Charlie began to converse at an early age because he was his mother's chief companion, and because he was exceptionally bright.

The couple planned to send the boy outdoors to help his father when he was a little older. It was a heavy load of work for one man, and the farm would be more productive when there were two. They intended to have many more sons and daughters.

A few months before the child's fourth birthday, his father developed a high fever and all-over pain that would not subside. There was no apothecary within twenty miles and the local midwife had no sort of treatment that could help him.

Sigrid knew nothing about medicine. As far as she knew, her husband died of a fever.

Family members were notified, but most of them couldn't arrive until days after his funeral. His sister and brother-in-law, Clara and Tyrone Overton, rode in from Teversall, where they ran a curio shop. To Sigrid, they were wealthy. Little Charlie marveled at their elegant Spanish horses and colorful clothing. The visit, overshadowed by deep grief, did afford the young couple a bright spot in being able to see the little boy for the first time, as they had no children of their own.

There were many painful questions to answer and problems to face.

"How will you manage?" the family asked Sigrid.

"I don't know," she replied. "But I shall. I can tend the fields. I can take care of the house. Charlie is getting older and he will just have to help me."

*Getting older,* Tyrone thought. *He is three years old.*

Before they left Rimmolan, Tyrone pulled Sigrid aside and handed her a bank note. "It's not much, but please remember that we are your family. If you need anything at all, send for us." He looked at the child. "I want my nephew to have a chance at a good life."

The statement hurt her deeply, but she understood. Tyrone was not related to her and Charlie was only his nephew by marriage. She appreciated his good heart.

After everyone left, Sigrid Blythe set about forging a new routine. The wheat field was the top priority. She had never done much farming herself, but she had been around it enough to know what needed to be done. She moved the workshop outdoors and young Charlie braided wheat alone while she hoed, weeded, irrigated, and tended to the field each day.

One day, as Charlie sat on a blanket that his mother had spread out on the lawn, a tremendously fat bumblebee-like insect flew out of the woodland beyond the east field and, in a straight line, advanced exactly to where he worked. It was furry and striped with silver and blue, rather than yellow and black. Its stinger appeared metallic, like a polished steel saber, and Charlie had no time at all to react to its approach before it landed on him, sending a wave of pain throughout his little arm. He swatted at it instinctively and it flew away without even leaving the stinger behind.

The boy screamed and ran toward his mother, who raced urgently toward him when she saw him clutching his arm. He was not a child who cried often.

The bee sting swelled to the size of a snapping turtle shell, which was easily the length from the boy's shoulder to his elbow. Sigrid picked him up and ran into the house, rinsing the sore lump with water and then packing it with a solution of bread and milk. She wrapped it up with a long strip of muslin and rocked him until the pain seemed to subside. "Was it a bee?" she asked him. "What bit you?"

"A blue bee," he replied, finally able to talk calmly. "A big blue bee."

Sigrid sighed. She would never know. She hoped it wasn't a spider. "Did the big blue bee fly to you?" She shot her hand toward him to simulate a bee. "Or did it walk?"

"It flew," he said. "The big blue bee flew very fast and stung me on my arm."

"It stung you. Did you see a stinger in your arm? Did you pull out a little black stick?"

"No," he said. "The stinger was like a sword."

She wished she had not told him about King Arthur just yet.

She wished that he didn't have to stay outside all day long.

The next morning, a small, strange-looking man arrived at the cottage. He walked around the outside of the house and stopped at the spot where Charlie laboriously struggled to plait straw with a sore arm. The man lifted up a long braided rope and raised his eyebrows. "Excellent work," he remarked, turning it from the shiny side to the dull side. "Did you do all of this?"

The boy nodded, absently. Praise meant nothing to him. The man would just buy it all and leave him to start all over on a new bundle.

Sigrid noticed their visitor and walked briskly from the field, wiping her hands on her apron. He smiled pleasantly as she approached. "Mrs. Blythe?"

"I am," she replied. "Would you like to order some straw?"

The man shook his head. "No, madam. I heard about your misfortune. I am very, very sorry. I am sure that the burden is very immense now that your husband is gone."

Sigrid looked at the boy, whose emotionless eyes remained fixed on his work. "It is rather manageable," she replied, lifting her chin and making it clear that she wanted the man to get to the point.

"I am Fenbeck," he said, removing his hat and taking a low bow. "I am looking for work. I would be happy to help you with your wheat field for a very reasonable wage."

Sigrid looked him up and down. He was nearly a foot shorter than she was, and she was not a tall woman. He was also scrawny. And pale skinned ... almost green. She couldn't imagine him able to do much farm work. "Thank you, sir, but I don't need help at this time. If you would like to leave me your name, I will keep it in mind in case I ever do need to hire someone."

He grinned, knowingly. "I'm aware that I don't have the physique of most excellent farmers, but I assure you that I am one of the best, and you would be amazed at how strong I actually am. Shall I demonstrate?"

Sigrid was amused by the image of him walking over to the barn and lifting it off the ground with one hand. "No, sir. That is quite all right. I do not doubt that you are strong."

He laughed. "I meant demonstrate, as in, work at no charge. For one week, so you can assess my skill."

"Why would you want to do that?"

Fenbeck sighed and lowered his head. "Mrs. Blythe, I have been having a very difficult time finding work ever since I arrived in this town. Nobody wants to hire me. I am sure that it is because I am too small, or too odd-looking. Perhaps my ears are too large."

He did have strangely-shaped ears, and he was the smallest grown man she had ever seen, but she was not one to judge anyone based on beauty. Her concern was that he would not be productive enough to make it worth paying him. How could he be? There was not a muscle to be found anywhere on his gaunt little frame.

However, if he was desperate enough to offer a week of work without pay, she was willing to take it. *As tired as I am, he could only be an improvement over what I could accomplish this week by myself,* she thought.

"Very well," she decided. "One week, but I have precious little money and cannot pay well. You would be wiser to seek employment with someone other than a poor widow, but if you would like to start tomorrow, that is fine with me."

It certainly was peculiar. Charlie watched the man constantly, beleaguered by his shrill voice and odd way of moving. He stared at Fenbeck's thin-lipped mouth, which overemphasized each syllable of every word. The boy also noted Fenbeck's wide amber eyes that seemed to see everything at once and rested several times on his small bandaged arm. When the strange creature left, Charlie watched his mother.

"Well, Charlie, I will be spending time with you for a few days. That will be nice!"

He agreed.

# Chapter 2

Fenbeck showed up at dawn wearing a maroon waist-coat and brown work pants. He removed the coat, underneath which he wore a tan shirt and an olive vest that was embroidered with zigzags of red, yellow, and blue. He carried a surprisingly beat-up tin lunch pail, which he set in a shady spot near the vegetable garden. The only tool he brought with him was a Dutch hoe with a long wooden handle and a pounded iron split blade.

Sigrid and Charlie could stay in the workroom that day— a nice break from the sun that was becoming rather oppressive as each July day passed. She waved through the window when he arrived, pitying him for looking the way he did. He went straight into the field and began to dig up the weeds between the rows of wheat, working from the front to the back of each earthen lane. Every time she peeked through the window, he was working. Maybe, if he didn't require much pay, he could actually be a help. It would be like having a large child working out there.

The stalks reached his waist, not a very impressive height, and she hoped to be able to harvest in August, in case September brought in an early freeze. Charles had always harvested in August and the current crop looked just as it normally looked in July. If she could just keep it healthy until then, they could survive through the winter on the earnings from it.

She repacked and changed the bandage on Charlie's arm, this time wrapping a smaller strip of muslin around it. The swelling had gone down considerably, but now he had a massive, hard, purplish-red bump that was still very tender. He still insisted that a blue bee had stung him. He called the stinger a dagger.

Sigrid offered Fenbeck a meal of bean soup and bread, but he declined, asking only for permission to help himself to the well when he needed a drink of water. As the sun began to set, he left his work and leaned the Dutch hoe against the side of the house. "I will see you again tomorrow, Mrs. Blythe," he said as he waved good-bye.

"Thank you, Mr. Fenbeck," she waved cheerfully.

When he was gone, she and Charlie walked out to inspect his work. The field was magnificent, with waving rows of wheat separated neatly by turned piles of earth. It looked as if ten people had worked on it that day.

The next morning, Fenbeck arrived again at sun-up. When he entered the field, the wheat reached his shoulders. *Is he ducking?* Sigrid watched for several minutes and each time he stood up, only his head rose above the golden stalks. Perhaps she had misjudged its height on the first day.

It rained that night.

On the third morning, Sigrid allowed herself to be astounded. She could not see the man's head at all. He could have left for the day and she wouldn't have known it.

Her mouth hung open in awe as she and Charlie walked out to the field and paced the end of it, glancing down each weed-free row until they found him, a few inches shorter than the general height of the crop. "Mr. Fenbeck, I am amazed. Look how high it is! And how thick!"

He planted the hoe firmly in front of him and put his hands on his hips. "I am glad you approve of my work, Mrs. Blythe."

"Approve! I have never seen wheat grow like this! Are you putting something on it? How did it double in size in just two days?"

He held his pleased expression. "I am just rather skilled at this," he said, grinning proudly and fixing his amber eyes on Charlie's bewildered face.

Unable to meet the strange man's gaze, Charlie shuddered and looked up at the grains, swaying high in the air from his perspective, and wondered if Fenbeck had a magic hoe. He knew that the abundance of wheat should only mean good things for his mother and himself, but somehow, it felt to him like a cautionary omen.

"Mrs. Blythe, if you don't mind my asking, what is your typical yield?"

"Usually forty or fifty bushels," she replied.

The smile remained. "Thank you."

*Thank you?* She was perplexed. The wheat was already higher than it had ever been at harvest time. By how much more did Fenbeck believe he could increase the yield? She decided not to ask just yet.

The next day, it was higher. Fenbeck carried buckets of water from the spring on the other side of the property and carefully irrigated every inch of the twenty-two acre field.

By the end of the week, the stalks stood at least six feet high. They bent dramatically with the weight of the enormous kernels. It was as dense as the bristles on a hairbrush. By all appearances, the wheat was ready to harvest.

Fenbeck worked throughout that last day, but before the sun began to set, Sigrid went out to the field to talk to him.

"I will have more wheat than I can handle," she laughed. "It will take me all winter just to split the straw for plaiting. I would like help, sir. Do you know how to use a chaff cutter?"

"I do," he said. "Are you willing to hire me?"

"Absolutely," she beamed. "And I will not tell anyone about you, because I wouldn't want to compete with anyone who had you working with their crops. Mr. Fenbeck, I cannot pay much now, but when this is all harvested, I will have a great deal more at my disposal."

"I trust you," he said. "Thank you, Mrs. Blythe. I will come every morning until the harvest is complete, the grains are separated … I can help with selling it as well, if you'd like."

"Oh, no. I can do that myself," she said, firmly.

They agreed that Fenbeck would continue to work and Sigrid would pay him what she could. She kept the matter completely to herself throughout all of it. While her family and neighbors believed her to be toiling the wheat herself and probably failing, she sat in the workroom, chatting pleasantly with Charlie as they plaited straw, just as things had been before Charles died.

She wondered, more than once, if Fenbeck was a blessing sent to help her. Perhaps Charles himself had made the arrangements from up in heaven. It didn't matter. She and Charlie were more than safe from the prospect of poverty and hunger.

On the eighth day, which was his first day as a paid employee, Fenbeck signaled for Sigrid to step outside before he began working. He rubbed his palms together and said, "Mrs. Blythe, I would like to ask you something."

"Of course, Mr. Fenbeck."

"I hope to save enough money to buy many thousands of acres of land in the north. I have noticed that your son, there … Charlie? How old is he?"

"Yes," she patted the boy's shoulder proudly. "He's three years old."

"He is incredibly skillful for being so young. I have never seen a baby that was able to plait straw before. It amazes me. He is a very promising little lad."

She smiled, but wondered where the topic was going.

"Mrs. Blythe, I would like to offer you a deal." He pinched his skeletal lips together. "If you yield a hundred bushels per acre or more, you will be rich."

"Quite rich," she agreed.

"If the yield is that high, I will not charge you anything for my work for five years. When little Charlie turns nine years old, I will take him to work with me for one year. He will be my apprentice and then, when the year is over, you will have a skilled wheat farmer at your home. Will you agree to that?"

As Sigrid thought about this business proposal, her eyes darted from the man's grinning mouth to the wheat field and back again. Only Fenbeck noticed the alarm on Charlie's face.

"Don't answer right now," he added pleasantly. "Tell me soon, though. I will work for pay, but I would rather teach your son what I know. It would be helpful for him to double my work for a year. Besides that, I have no son to pass my knowledge to. It would be nice to be able to train a youth to grow wheat. When I die, I do not want this method to die with me."

One hundred bushels per acre. It was more than she could fathom. She had never heard of anyone yielding more than fifty. But why wouldn't he just tell her his secrets regarding wheat farming? Why did he have to take an apprentice?

Moreover, why Charlie?

Despite her reservations, Sigrid was certain that she would be a fool to pass up the opportunity to have six-foot-high wheat every year. That evening, before Fenbeck left, she told him that she would take him up on his offer.

It was a deal.

# Chapter 3

Sigrid and Charles had hoped to save enough money to purchase a mechanical reaper within the next few years. As it stood, she had only an old scythe, but Fenbeck didn't seem to expect anything more advanced than that. Sigrid arranged for a traveling work crew to arrive with a threshing machine when the wheat was cut, guessing that it would take about ten days to harvest. It was twenty-two heavily-laden acres and only two small field workers.

She followed Fenbeck to the field with a sickle in her hand, but he turned around and said, "You should go and sweep out the barn. We are going to have a great deal to fit in there."

"Don't you want me to help with the reaping?"

"I don't think so. Just get the barn ready and I can do this."

Bewildered, she took Charlie's hand and did what Fenbeck had suggested. It seemed foolish to sweep the barn now, when it would probably be weeks before any of the wheat was ready for storage, but if he just wanted to work alone, she would let him.

Sigrid and Charlie cleaned the barn. They tended the chickens. They weeded the vegetable garden. Charlie asked, "Will the man bring his magic hoe to the vegetable garden?"

*Not a bad idea,* Sigrid thought, but she felt obligated to correct him. "Charlie, there is no magic. He doesn't have a magic hoe. He is just a very, very good farmer."

He shook his blond head. "He's a magic farmer."

How would he know? The little boy didn't remember the wheat field from a year earlier. The three-year-old had no frame of reference regarding much of anything. Yet, he maintained the position, and Sigrid found it quite impossible to disagree.

She went into the cottage and started a big pot of stew, complete with freshly-dug potatoes and carrots. She hoped that it was something Fenbeck would eat. Somehow, he seemed like someone who didn't eat normal food and she hadn't caught a glimpse of any of his packed meals up close. Still, she hoped that the gesture would suffice.

At noon, she opened the kitchen door to offer him a bowl of stew.

"Oh, my goodness!" She shrieked, grabbing onto the door handle to keep from falling over. She threw her other hand over her mouth and ceased to breathe for several seconds while Charlie scrambled behind her and peeked through the doorway.

All of the wheat was cut. The field was completely leveled with pyramid-shaped bushels already drying in the sun.

When Charles Senior and three or four of his friends used to cut the wheat together, they would manage to reap two or three acres per day, yet this frail looking, four-foot-tall man had cut twenty-two acres in less than six hours.

Fenbeck was seated in the grass near the doorstep, his knees bent and drawn up to his chin, his hands grasping his crossed ankles. "Send for the thresher," he grinned.

"How? What? Mr. Fenbeck, this is a *miracle!*"

Charlie didn't know what a miracle was, but the tone in his mother's voice confirmed his suspicions. Fenbeck could not be human. The menacing smirks and endless deal-making led Charlie to believe that Fenbeck wasn't even good, whatever he … or *it* … was. His mother, however, was all business. If Fenbeck was able to make them rich, Sigrid could not imagine him capable of doing anything wrong. Charlie could only hope that something else would come along and stop this string of events that didn't feel right to him.

"Not a miracle, Mrs. Blythe."

Sigrid forgot about the stew. She wondered if Charles Senior could see this. She wondered if he had anything to do with it. It was, indeed, a miracle. She dropped to her knees and began to pray feverishly.

Later, as they ate the stew, Fenbeck reminded her of their agreement.

"Mrs. Blythe, how many bushels of wheat do you suspect you have out there?"

She glanced through the window, which only allowed her a view of one corner of the field. The piles were much closer together than they had been on previous years. "Why, I don't know," she replied. "Do you?"

"Well over two thousand," he said. "Well over a hundred bushels per acre."

She looked at Charlie, who seemed to be contentedly spooning the rich beef broth into his mouth. If her son learned how to farm from this man he would enjoy a very comfortable life, but part of the whole story made her felt uneasy. The *magic hoe* part. The *giant wheat* part. Something other than farming skills had been at work.

Sigrid wondered if he could thresh all of it himself with a flail just as easily, but she had not asked him to do that as she felt that he had done enough. She sent for the thresher and a crew arrived the next day, issuing a collective gasp upon realizing how tall the wheat had stood.

They separated the grain at the head of each stalk from the straw. Then, they piled it into bales and filled seemingly endless sacks with the enormous kernels of grain.

Sigrid could hear the workers exclaim at the size of the crop and hoped that they wouldn't haggle with her. She had agreed to pay them their standard per-acre price and that was what she intended to pay.

She felt rich. She saved enough seed for the following year and sold all of the sacks of grain that she wouldn't need, easily earning enough money to live on for more than three years. She could never plait that much straw in a year. She didn't need to continue straw plaiting at all with the money she had, but she wanted to earn more. She sold most of the straw.

Fenbeck refused payment several times, but Sigrid insisted that he take something. The promise of an apprentice in six years did not seem like nearly enough. She bought him a little white Welsh Mountain pony and sent it home with him the next time he dropped by. After that, she did not see him for eight months.

She wondered if he would return and rather doubted it, but she and Charlie lived well over the winter with the pantry well stocked, plenty of firewood, and they even enjoyed a few imported extravagances like cinnamon and white sugar. They braided straw throughout the fall and winter, bringing in more money. She did not like to sew, so she purchased ready-made clothing from the store. She had new bonnets for herself, new shoes for both of them, and there was still money left over.

One day the following July, Fenbeck arrived at the Blythes' doorstep on the back of his Welsh pony. Sigrid had already turned the opposite field, sown the seeds, pulled weeds, and tended it all as well as she could. The wheat was about two feet high. After Fenbeck spent a week hoeing, it was again six feet tall and heavily weighted with massive grain kernels. He cut and bundled it, the threshers separated it, and the Blythes lived lavishly (by their standards) for another year.

It was the same the next year. And the next. And the next.

Throughout the summer during which Charlie was eight years old, his mother spent less time than usual in the workroom with him and much more time corresponding and practicing domestic skills like napkin-folding and tea-serving. She told him that she was refreshing her skills as a proper hostess, as she intended to ask family members to visit after the harvest.

Writing letters was not an occupation that came naturally to her. "Charlie," she called to him one morning, "how would you spell 'draperies?'"

The boy hadn't seen that word in any of the books he had read, but he replied, "D-R-A-P ..." He thought about it. Was a draper someone who draped? Perhaps it was the term for a person who crafted window coverings. He decided to venture a guess. "… E-R-I-E-S. That is how I would spell it. It might not be correct. What are you writing?"

"A letter," she said, offering no further details. After a moment, Charlie stopped plaiting and turned toward the window, through which he could see the field, high and full as it usually was in mid-summer. The boy could not remember their own crop ever looking like the sparse fields he and his mother passed on their way to town in midsummer.

Fenbeck was in there somewhere among the heavy blades of wheat. Somehow, the man had been able to keep his methods a secret for five years. Charlie had remembered everything he could, but when he tried to put it together, he could come up with no rational reason for Fenbeck to be there.

Sigrid appeared in the doorway. "Charlie, why aren't you working? Do you feel all right?"

"Yes, Mother. I was just trying to make sense of Fenbeck."

Sigrid forced out a dismissive chuckle. "That is not a worthwhile way to spend your time."

"Perhaps not, but I just can't help it," he replied. Each time he had tried to express his concerns to his mother, she had laughed it off. Great fortune was, to her, worth the doubt and uncertainty that often accompanied it. "Mother, if I was an odd-looking boy with no home or family, but I could grow wheat the way he does, would I spend five years working for someone else? Of course not! I would start my own farm and do whatever I pleased with the money."

"Anyone with a grain of common sense would," she agreed.

"So Fenbeck has no common sense?"

Sigrid pressed her lips together. Charlie sighed. Fenbeck was obviously much smarter than anyone they knew. As much as Charlie loved his mother and wanted her life to be easy and enjoyable, he couldn't stop himself from wanting to chastise her for her greed. Sigrid was a bright woman, though not formally educated. He had always respected her for her strength and willingness to accept fate, as painful as it was at times. She had never pitied herself or resented women whose husbands were still alive. Still, whenever Sigrid met with an opportunity to have more, she seemed far too quick to abandon her convictions.

"Charlie, this is what is keeping us alive," she said, and she left the room to return to her desk. Charlie picked up his roll of straw and continued working.

In the sitting room, Sigrid put down her quill and bit her lip to keep herself from crying. She had not yet told her son that she had agreed to his impending apprenticeship and now, knowing that Charlie mistrusted Fenbeck as much as she did, she deeply regretted that agreement.

They had no relatives living nearby. She didn't even have any friends who she would feel comfortable asking for help. Only one thought offered her a bit of comfort and a sliver of hope: she had a great deal of money saved. Anyone with a fortune can bargain their way out of anything.

"Mr. Fenbeck," she began when he arrived at her home that July. "I have determined that I cannot spare Charlie for a year. You know I am a widow. I need his assistance around the farm. Name a sum of money and I will give it to you instead."

Fenbeck was clearly incredulous. His thin-lipped mouth expanded like a rubber band in every direction as he articulated each syllable. "I told you that I do not want money. I earn money all year long. You made an agreement with me and I gave you five magnificent harvests."

"Yes, and I am willing to pay you." Then, she remembered that he had no use for money. But he did. The reason he had wanted an apprentice in the first place was supposedly to help him earn enough money to buy land in the north. Why wouldn't he take her money? "Mr. Fenbeck, please. I did not sign anything."

"But you gave me your word."

Somehow, his eyes were capable of narrowing angrily while bulging out of his face. It frightened her and she was glad that, as far as she knew, Charlie was not in the yard to see and hear any of it. She took a deep breath and stood tall above him to let him know that she was not going to be intimidated. "I did," she said, "but I am afraid that I must break it. I cannot spare him."

He stood, buggy-eyed with puffed cheeks, for several minutes, absorbing the unpleasant news. Then he lifted a knotted index finger into the air and wrinkled his nose. He had a new idea.

"I will excuse him under one condition." He continued to hold his finger up and smiled as if he were the most eligible bachelor in all the land. "You shall marry me and have two helpers on the farm year-round."

Sigrid's stomach turned and she shuddered. "Absolutely not! How dare you!"

He scowled angrily. "That is your choice. I will work in the field today and I expect an answer by sundown. Marry me this week or Charlie must go with me."

# Chapter 4

**C**harlie was upstairs at the time, reading a book about botany. His mother's most extravagant splurge had been on books for their home, a luxury that neither of his parents knew as children. Indeed, she had taught him how to read, but at age eight, he was already a stronger reader than anyone else in Rimmolan. His parents had grown up with only an almanac and a few storybooks. Sigrid proudly made a production of taking Charlie to pick out books of his very own. The book on botany was of particular interest to the boy because he was determined to learn for himself whatever it was that Fenbeck knew about plants.

He heard them talking outside, but not well enough to understand many of their words. When he glanced through the window, he saw a sneering glare on Fenbeck's face that made him wish that he had listened. His mother might need him, even if she wouldn't listen to him.

He closed his book and went downstairs to find his mother frowning in the kitchen; the man having just departed for the wheat field.

Sigrid was shrewd when it came to business. She had always handled the arrangements for selling and buying items, while Charles had produced the items that she sold and used the items that she bought. As difficult as it was to get through life as a widow, she had a strong business mentality in her favor.

Fenbeck's ultimatum, however, confounded her. She definitely would not marry him and she would not allow him to take Charlie for a year. This meant that she would no longer make giant profits from her wheat harvest unless she could find some other way to convince him to continue working for her.

Could she tell him that Charlie would work as his apprentice when he turned fifteen? Eighteen? Of course not. Charlie had no such inclination and it wouldn't be fair for her to use him in that way. *I have been such a fool,* she scolded herself.

Before sundown, she refused the proposal and Fenbeck left in a fury. Sigrid and Charlie, now a big enough boy to assist with some of the heavier farm work, set out to the fields and tended them by themselves. There would be no early harvest this year.

She dispatched a letter to Teversall and another to Hallam … just in case.

The wheat was two feet high that day. It was two feet high a week later. It grew to three feet by the end of August. It would be enough to live on. Sigrid contracted a crew of local country boys to arrive the following Tuesday and cut the wheat. She did not bother yet to contact the local men who operated the town's only threshing machine, as its use would not be needed for quite some time.

Then, on Monday morning, Sigrid woke at dawn and did the first thing she did every day. She looked through the kitchen window toward the wheat field.

It was gone.

It was not trampled. It was not destroyed. All of the wheat was literally gone; a twenty-two-acre rectangle of brown soil stretched flat across her property.

Someone had come and dug it all up.

She truly did think it was a nightmare, at first. She didn't make a sound, but smacked herself sharply on the forearm, hoping to wake up.

It was no dream, and there was only one person who could have silently cleared out an entire wheat field in a few hours. Fenbeck must have been back, and he might not be satisfied with merely destroying her crop. He had made it clear that he wanted either her hand in marriage or the apprenticeship of the boy. One or the other.

At that moment, she knew that her last-resort plans must be implemented. She held back tears as she explained to her son in a hushed tone, "Charlie, we have to leave Rimmolan. Fenbeck wants you for his apprentice. I will not allow it. If you do not go with him, he wants me to marry him."

"Mother, I will go," he said, horrified at the thought of his mother marrying Fenbeck.

"I just said that I will not allow it. We have nothing to gain and much to lose from you going with him. Now, go and pack a few things for yourself. I will tell you where you are going when we get into the coach. Your name is no longer Charlie."

He couldn't believe it. "Mother, *I* am going? What is going to happen to you?"

"Our crop is ruined. I am going to take a domestic position at the home of a duke. Don't worry, son. I will come for you as soon as it seems safe. I do not know what this man is capable of. We have to act immediately."

She grabbed a pair of sewing shears and cut the boy's hair so short that he almost appeared bald. She handed him his largest hat. She obscured herself in dark clothing and a full bonnet. They took a few items and pretended to be headed toward the market, lest Fenbeck should see them.

Of course, he did.

They walked through town and headed toward the post office, where Sigrid mailed a letter to her next-door neighbor (which undoubtedly seemed odd to the postmaster), paid their fare, and they quickly boarded the mail coach. When it left the station, Sigrid let out an enormous sigh and a tear fell down her cheek. It appeared as though they had made it.

Fenbeck followed a half-mile behind the coach, riding his white Welsh pony. He didn't know where they were going, but calculated that they couldn't possibly know anyone who lived too far away. These were simple country people. He assumed that he would follow them to the next town, or possibly the town after that.

He wasn't that far off. Teversall was only about forty miles away.

Charlie sat by the window and watched the landscape change subtly as they left the only town he had even known. The road was little more than a worn path through the forest, but it all seemed foreign to him; it seemed entirely possible that he could be leaving Rimmolan forever.

His eyes stopped on a bright blue light that suddenly emerged from the forest. It might have resembled a firefly if one that bright and large had existed. It appeared to have two legs, almost like a human. It darted out from between the trees and disappeared behind the wagon.

He decided not to tell his mother. She still enjoyed teasing him about the blue bumblebee that he claimed stung him when he was three years old, and she was too distraught at the moment to care.

The blue light hovered in the air when the coach passed from its view, and sent a shower of tiny flickering filaments toward the ground. The road began to change and soon became completely distorted. The trail that the coach was on disappeared and a new one swerved to the left, eventually connecting to another road that led to towns far removed from Teversall and Hallam.

Long before the angry little man on the white pony arrived at that spot, the blue light was gone. Fenbeck followed the road for fifty miles before he realized that he had lost track of the mail coach.

# Chapter 5

Most people—if they believe in fairies at all—think that there is one type of creature called a *fairy*, but that couldn't be further from the truth. Each forest throughout the land has its own unique population of fairies, and it is rare to find a forest without such magical beings. The enchanted little societies keep to themselves, for the most part, and each civilization has, above all, its own set of rules.

In some forests, the fairies are entirely benevolent and help the gnomes to protect and maintain the natural surroundings of their environment. In some forests, the fairies are quite the opposite and play mean-spirited tricks on the humans, animals, and even on each other. In many forests, the fairies are good to other fairies and the living things within the forest, but they like to meddle with the human population in the neighboring town.

The fairies that resided in the woodland outskirts of Rimmolan represented a combination of the first and last types. They were kind, absolutely. They never argued, never complained, and never tried to take more than their share of anything. They helped the gnomes to heal wounded animals and nurture troubled plants. However, being fairies, they could not help but seek to impress each other with their magic every now and then.

These particular sprites generally took the form of insects whenever they left the forest. Most commonly, they disguised themselves as fireflies, as this was a small, efficient form that could accentuate the brilliant color of their tone. In the event that a fairy was traveling further than a few miles from its tree, it would often take the form of a bird.

Thea's tone was blue. It suited her well. She was a clear thinker, always calm, and completely honest. According to the rules, she was allowed to cast spells on the local humans who also had blue tones within her assigned birth range. Little Charlie Blythe was one of her humans.

The fairies rarely cast spells, although they were free to do so. This particularly wise society in Rimmolan generally thought it best to leave the humans alone. Thea tried to do that, but her heart was touched when she saw Charlie at age three, toiling at straw plaiting all day long like an adult. Then, when his father died, she felt that she had to do something for him.

As humans know, the most precious gifts usually require some measure of pain. She hated to do it, but she was determined to give Charlie a bit of fairy magic … just enough so that he could use it when his troubles were almost more than he could bear. Disguised as a bee, she left the forest and stung him on the arm, ensuring him a lifetime of unwavering inner strength. What better gift could anyone receive?

Fenbeck had witnessed this. Somehow, he had evaded her perception and she didn't realize it until she flew back into the woods. He had seen her flying toward the Blythe home and he had followed her. And it couldn't have been worse. He was a Borgh elf.

From that day forth, Thea considered it her personal responsibility to keep Charlie safe from Fenbeck. When he and his mother fled Rimmolan she kept watch, and when she saw Fenbeck following the mail coach, she diverted him.

If she hadn't cared so much in the first place, that evil Borgh elf never would have shown up at the Blythes' doorstep, never would have conjured up that scheme with the wheat field, and never would have forced Charlie and his mother to abandon their home and each other. She felt awful, but she was afraid to cast another large spell. The outcome could be even worse.

Fairies are often reckless. They mean well, but seldom consider consequences. The more sensitive fairies, like Thea, often suffer because of it, and ultimately resolve to leave the humans alone.

She did not live in a sheltered dwelling as many of the other fairies did. The fairies in Rimmolan were actually dryads, each living in a particular tree. After tricking Fenbeck into going the wrong way, Thea was tired, and she retreated to her birch bough for the rest of the day, hoping that Charlie would make it to his new life in good spirits. But from her favorite limb, she cast one more spell, in honor of a society of fairies that lived far away in a land called Brudovel, a neighboring town to Charlie's destination, Teversall.

This fairy society resided in a meadow covered with Mariposa lilies, and their dwelling resembled an enormous upturned flower. They were known among the fairies for being partial to anything flower-related. Charlie had been reading a book on the subject just days earlier and Thea knew that she could influence him with little trouble.

From deep within the tree she whispered, "Call yourself *Calyx* and you will find yourself favored by the fairies in your new land."

In the coach, the boy turned to his mother, who had refrained from saying his name since they left their home roughly disguised. "Mother, I am now Calyx," he said.

The other two passengers in the coach were asleep. Sigrid thought he had been dreaming. "Get some rest, sweetheart. You are going to stay with your Aunt Clara and Uncle Tyrone in Teversall."

"I like the word *Calyx*, the part of a plant that holds in the petals. Call me Calyx."

Now she understood, and was filled with pride at her son's wisdom and tenacity. She knew that he would get through this ordeal triumphantly. At eight years old, he was able to give himself a pseudonym. She wrapped her arm around him and whispered very quietly, "If you like it, then so do I, but never forget who you really are."

"Never," he said. "A name is just a word."

"Indeed."

They rode on for a while and she thought of names for herself, but recoiled when she realized that she was not nearly as strong as the little boy beside her. She wanted to remain Sigrid Blythe. She wanted to go back to her cozy life in Rimmolan. She wanted Charles back. She wanted to raise her son. It all began to sink in and she feared that she might break down if she continued pondering pseudonyms for herself, so she stared out the window with her arm around her Charlie … or Calyx … and tried to think about nothing at all.

# Chapter 6

Welcome to Teversall

The coach stopped at the Teversall post office the following afternoon. Though they had dozed throughout much of the ride, Sigrid and Calyx were exhausted from having endured so many hours of constant jarring. They were also emotionally fatigued, of course.

Clara and Tyrone Overton had spotted the coach as it made its way through town and they rushed over to the station to pick up their guests. Although they lived in town, just two blocks away, they took the coach to accommodate the Blythes' luggage, if they had any.

They had one bag apiece, and could have carried them without much trouble, but the thoughtful gesture lifted Sigrid's spirits. Calyx did not feel like climbing into another horse-drawn vehicle right away, but he was glad that it was a very short ride, and he was even gladder to see family members who could help them.

He knew that Teversall was larger than Rimmolan, but he was nonetheless surprised. He was accustomed to Rimmolan's dirt roads and its vastness. No two buildings were close together in Rimmolan, not even downtown. Here, the marketplace consisted of a long strip paved with large, flat stones, with a dozen or more shops on each side of it. Most of the buildings looked rather new, or at least freshly painted. The people, generally rustic and simple like the people in Rimmolan, seemed far more motivated to get to wherever they were going, and Calyx was relieved, for their sakes, that the buildings were not too far apart.

Tyrone, a tall, slender man with shiny dark wafts of hair jutting from beneath his grey bowler hat, smiled affably as he drove the carriage with Calyx on the box beside him, and the two women sat in the seats behind them. "We are very pleased to have you with us," Tyrone told Calyx in a pleasant but grave voice. "I know this will be a difficult adjustment for you. Don't hesitate to tell us what we can do to make it easier. Aunt Clara will say the same thing ... probably hundreds of times."

Calyx tried to smile. He hardly knew these people. He wanted to know where his mother would be, and when he could look forward to living with her again. "Thank you, Uncle Tyrone."

Tyrone's voice brightened. "What would you like first? We have a room for you, but what would you like in it? What do you enjoy doing?"

He didn't even know. Calyx stared at the people along the road, carrying goods in and out of the stores. *They all must have had bumper crops this year,* he thought.

Just then, Sigrid bent forward and poked Calyx on the shoulder. "Oh, look, Char ... Calyx: a library!"

Rimmolan had no library, which was why Sigrid had spent so much money on books. Calyx stared at the three-story stone building with crisp white painted trim around the door and windows. He had heard of libraries, but did not think that there were many in the world. "How many books are in the library?" he asked Tyrone.

The man smiled broadly. "Oh, many hundreds, I imagine. I am not sure. Would you like to walk there with me tomorrow morning and find out?"

Calyx nodded. Teversall was rather overwhelming, but to be able to walk to a place where there were hundreds of books would be a very attractive benefit. There were so many things that he wanted to know.

"He loves to read," Sigrid told Clara, and then her voice dropped. "I hope he continues."

"He will," Clara assured her, smiling with serene compassion as she patted Sigrid's arm. "I'm so glad that you taught him to read. We have a schoolhouse here too, you know. When the summer is over, he can go to school. It sounds like he will have no trouble keeping up with the others. We could even hire a tutor rather than send him to school, but perhaps the company of other youngsters would be good for him."

*School?* Calyx had never given a thought to the prospect of going to school. He wasn't sure whether he liked the idea or not. Mostly, he did.

The carriage stopped in front of an enormous, handsome white manor with an abundance of windows and dark green shutters with little pine tree shapes that had been cut out of them. Giant pillars rose from the endless front porch to the upper floor.

A pathway made of round red stones led them from the carriage to the front door. It was the closest thing that Calyx had ever seen to a palace.

A footman in dark grey trousers and a black collarless jacket adorned with about twenty brass buttons running in a straight line up the front took all of their bags and waited for them to enter the house. Tyrone introduced him as "Arthur."

Calyx had read enough about civilized culture to know that most wealthy masters called their footmen either "James" or "John" regardless of their real names. He smiled kindly at Arthur, comforted by this indication that his uncle and aunt valued their servants' individuality.

The housekeeper, Eleanor, opened the door for them and greeted the Blythes as if they were visiting her own home. Calyx then learned that she did live there. He took a deep breath to avoid becoming dizzy. *There are so many people in this house!*

There was a cook named Meredith and a scullery maid named Helen. There were probably more. Calyx wondered if his aunt and uncle had to do anything for themselves, and wished that his mother could live the same way.

They had offered. Sigrid would not allow it. She knew that they did not need another housekeeper or servant of any sort and she did not wish to put them out any further. She could make good money working for the Duke of Hallam and as soon as she could, she would return to Teversall. In the meantime, she wanted Calyx to have an education and reap the benefits of living with the good Overtons.

Furthermore, she thought it best for them to remain apart until the possibility of Fenbeck finding them was diminished. Calyx no longer had his longer, straw-colored hair. It was cropped very short and it appeared almost light brown. He would grow and change over the next few years and it would be difficult to recognize him. He was safer without her.

She told her son all of this, so he would not resent the Overtons.

Arthur took Calyx's things to an upstairs room that was carpeted and decorated with olive-colored wallpaper in a subtle leaf pattern. He had never slept in a room with wallpaper before. He stared at it for an hour before he went to bed that night and wondered how many bundles of pleated straw it would cost to put fancy paper on the walls. Sitting upon the high brass-framed bed, his feet barely touched the soft, brown carpet. He felt guilty for enjoying any of it.

Sigrid entered the room to say goodnight.

"I will be leaving tomorrow," she said. "I will write as soon as I get to Hallam."

"Yes, Mother."

"I am very, very proud of you, Charlie. Very proud. Your father would be, too. You are a strong, smart, wonderful little boy. It will be good for you to be here with the Overtons."

"Mother, I don't care about having fancy carpets and people waiting on me. I would rather be back in the country, running the farm."

"I know," she said. "So would I. But we cannot take the chance. You will adjust."

Calyx didn't completely understand why they were running away from Fenbeck. The little man was barely taller than he was, and much scrawnier. Someone that size normally wouldn't stand a chance against Sigrid *or* Calyx. How was he such a threat? But deep inside, he knew that Fenbeck was capable of doing some amazing things. If he wanted to hurt them, he probably could.

"Mother, I am going to work toward one goal. I am going to take care of … of *him* and make sure that he can never bother you again."

"Hush!" She covered his mouth. "You must never talk about him. Not even to me. Do you understand that? Never. He will move on, unfortunately to someone else, but he will forget about us eventually. We just need to stay quiet for a while."

But Calyx was serious. "Yes, Mother, but I really meant that."

Sigrid smiled lovingly. "I know. But you cannot let your heart be filled with bitterness. If you do, then he has won. Don't be bitter, Charlie. I'm not."

# Chapter 7

igrid Blythe left Teversall the next morning, stoic and noble, allowing neither herself nor her son to shed a tear. She knew many respectable young women who had become housemaids and she was not too proud to join them, although the notion that giving Calyx to his aunt and uncle would improve his life did hurt her pride.

Yet, she knew that it would.

And she had lied. She *was* bitter. She had sent that eleventh-hour letter to her neighbors, asking them to take the chickens and the vegetables (if Fenbeck had not also destroyed the vegetables) and to contact her sister so she could claim the house. It would not be lost to the family, but Sigrid mourned for her own losses, already far too numerous for someone her age.

She took solace, however, in knowing that Calyx would have plenty to eat, a nice home to live in, a school to attend, and many other advantages that she never had as a child. She tried to focus on that as the distance between them grew further.

Calyx saw the library that morning. Tyrone watched his eyes with fascination as he scanned the first room, reading the title of every book on each shelf. The librarian, Mr. Duffy, noticed the new boy and rushed over to them.

"Good morning, Mr. Overton! Do we have a guest?"

"A resident, actually," Tyrone replied, shaking his hand. "Mr. Duffy, this is my nephew, Calyx Overton. He has come to live with us."

Calyx Overton. It sounded so strange. *I am Charles Blythe,* the boy thought. Why had his uncle given him their last name so quickly? *It is strange how quickly someone can become an entirely different person.*

Mr. Duffy looked at Calyx sympathetically, assuming exactly what they were telling people: that his parents were both dead. "It is very nice to meet you," he said, now shaking Calyx's hand. "What a fine-looking lad this one is! I hope to see you in here a great deal."

"I intend to read most of these books," Calyx told him. "Probably not all of them, though."

Both men laughed. "Probably not," Tyrone replied. "This is only one room. I will have to teach you how it is all set up, so that you can find what you are looking for. We must get over to the shop soon, so perhaps later. Would you like to pick a book or two to take with you now?"

Calyx nodded. Mr. Duffy said, "Mr. Overton, I would be honored to spend a half an hour showing him the library, if that would be helpful. This afternoon would be fine, or tomorrow."

"A professional tour!" Tyrone exclaimed. "That would be very kind of you. Would you like to come back this afternoon, Calyx?"

He nodded. He had no idea what activities would be filling his days. He didn't even know what the plans were for this day, other than seeing Tyrone's store, but he knew that he could find out practically anything in the library and he looked forward to answering as many of his own questions as he could.

"I will send him over around two o'clock, if that would work well for you," Tyrone said.

Mr. Duffy nodded and smiled. "Brilliant. I will get a card ready for him."

*Send him over?* Calyx had never walked into a public building by himself in his life. In Rimmolan, they lived quite far from the town center and Sigrid was always with him when they shopped. Sometimes she would go alone, but he never did.

When they reached the front of Overton's Curios, he understood why. The library was right across the street.

"Here we are," Tyrone said, holding the door and ushering Calyx into the front of the shop with his other hand on the boy's shoulder. "'O's Curios,' they call it. This is where I spend most of my time. I would like you to help here. Would that appeal to you?"

Calyx's eyes were in constant motion. The entire store was filled with things that his mother could never afford, even when she was rich. The large room was arranged in aisles, each displaying a completely different type of product. In the front, there were household goods ranging from rolled oriental rugs and silk cushions to fireplace tools and hat racks. One side of the store displayed shelves of pottery and exquisitely-detailed oil lamps. The other was lined by a glass-enclosure, protecting smaller, more expensive items like jewelry, watches, silverware, and gold-plated cups and scissors. Throughout the rest of the shop there were toys, ornamental hats, writing tools, musical instruments, mechanical gadgets, vases, toiletry items, and many things that Calyx could not even categorize. He had never seen so much in one place before and was quite sure that he could stand in one spot all day long without failing to find something new to look at.

"I would like to help," he said, imagining himself showing the customers exactly what they were looking for. Whatever it was, it must be here.

Several customers were already in the store, and Tyrone greeted them. Two employees were there to answer questions, but Tyrone liked to be present much of the time in case the shop did not carry a particular item. He had connections all over the world and could get just about anything.

Calyx wondered if his mother had ever seen O's Curios. She was always so good with business matters; he was sure that she could run a shop like this.

He walked to the back with his uncle, who cheerfully proceeded to wedge open a number of enormous wooden pallets. "I have a gift for you," he said. "I think it might be in this one from Geneva." He pulled out arms full of brown paper padding and inspected a few items. "The most interesting items usually come from Geneva," he said, as if he were already training Calyx for the business.

"Really, Uncle?"

"Oh, yes. They make machines there. Not work machines like you have seen on the farm, but small machines that do fascinating things. I am going to give you one if I can find it."

Calyx stood shoulder to shoulder with his uncle, who was bent over the box, sifting through the endless quantity of wrapped items.

"I think this might be it." Tyrone squeezed something small, flat, and round and then removed the paper that covered it. "Will you look at this? Brilliant! Here, Calyx."

It was a gleaming gold pocket watch with a smooth glass cover atop elegant black Roman numerals. He held it in his hand and stared at it as if it were alive.

"Can you tell time?" Tyrone asked him.

"Yes. Thank you, Uncle, but this ..."

"I want you to have it. You can carry it in your pocket so that you will never be late for anything. Punctuality is very important, you know."

Calyx's steel-blue eyes glanced from the watch to Tyrone's face. He couldn't remember ever having to be on time for anything. "Thank you very much. I—I cannot believe how small it is. And thin. I've seen pocket watches, but they are always so much bigger and heavier. How did they fit all the ... whatever it is ... into this little case?"

"Isn't it wonderful?" Tyrone was surprised and pleased that his nephew was so full of wonder. He had assumed that a boy who had lived an unvaried life on the farm with few companions would be rather dull-witted. Not the case here.

Calyx asked questions about everything. The Overtons had an atlas at their home and he referred to it so often that they began to keep it in his room. He wanted to know where every item in the curio shop came from, and then he had to find that place on a map. After he found it, he looked at the other places around it, and read what the atlas said about that region of the world. Tyrone and Clara often joked that Calyx must have every word of that atlas memorized, and he practically did, after a while.

He went to the stables once or twice a week and the groom taught him to ride on their smallest Norfolk Trotter. He liked the way the horses ran across the fenced meadow as if they were completely free, yet remained resigned to the fact that they were dependent on humans. It was a good mix and they seemed happy.

Tyrone and Clara applied the same principle to the way they raised Calyx. He was free to visit shops, read in his room, explore the store, run around the yard, see the horses or chat with the house staff, as long as he also did what was expected.

The calluses that had covered his fingers and especially his thumbs since he was three years old eventually disappeared. He did not have chores around the house and he certainly didn't have to plait straw, clean a chicken coop, or weed a garden. All the Overtons required him to do was to spend at least two pleasant hours a day at Overton's Curios, assisting the employees and the customers.

The people around town began to come into the store just to meet the sociable, blue-eyed, little boy who knew everything about each item. He made friends, and sometimes he would go to the park in the afternoon and play with them.

When Calyx arrived at the schoolhouse that fall, the schoolmaster of the middle class (which was populated with students of about Calyx's age who could read) greeted him and told him to sit in the front row. "You may need some extra help until you have caught up with the others," he explained. He set a spelling book on the desk in front of the boy. "Mr. Overton tells me that you can already read. That is good. This class is up to three-syllable words. If that is too much for you, I would be happy to work with you in order to avoid placing you with the younger children."

"I can spell many three-syllable words," Calyx replied politely.

The schoolmaster nodded. "In mathematics, we are going to begin to learn our multiplication tables, but you must have a firm grasp of addition and subtraction."

"I can multiply," Calyx said.

"Lad, I understand that you might have a certain amount of pride at stake, but if you have lived in the country without a tutor or any schooling, that is nothing to be ashamed of. Nobody here will laugh at you. I promise."

Again, Calyx smiled politely, but the schoolmaster saw a flash of confident amusement. "What is seven times eight?"

"Fifty-six."

The schoolmaster raised his eyebrows. "What is twenty-five times ten?"

"Two hundred and fifty."

A grin crossed the scholar's face. "What, Mr. Overton, is the square root of seven hundred and eighty-four?"

"Square root, sir? I apologize. I don't think I've gotten that far."

"A square root is the number that is multiplied by itself to give you the product. For instance, the square root of sixteen is four."

"I see." Calyx pressed his lips together. "Twenty-eight."

At this, the schoolmaster beamed. "Nine years old with no formal education," he mused to himself. "I apologize, lad. In fact, I would like to keep you aside. While the others are studying, I'm going to give you the end-of-year exam and admit you to the advanced class."

Calyx did not have to study to get good grades. He did not have to work to make people like him. Most things came naturally to him because he enjoyed being a part of everything.

Clara wrote a letter to Sigrid, singing his praises. She and Tyrone had no children of their own, but she couldn't imagine having one more agreeable than Calyx. Her heart ached to think how Sigrid must miss him. He had only been in Teversall a few months and they already felt as if they wouldn't know what to do without him.

# Chapter 8

Over the next few years, Calyx's position at Overton's Curios grew increasingly prominent. He went there after school each day, and even when he was as young as ten some customers would wait until the afternoon to visit the store, just so that he could be the one to answer their questions.

One day, a shipment arrived from China. Tyrone Overton's face lit up as he held the door for the porter, who wheeled the crate to the back of the store. "Calyx," he beamed, "look at these!" He pried open the box and pulled out an oddly-shaped, bulky iron object with one hand. It looked like two coarsely-made goblets fused together without any stems or bases. With his other hand, Tyrone remove two long sticks, connected by a long piece of twine, from of the crate. He held all of this out to Calyx.

"What are they" Calyx inquired, taking them.

"It's called a *diabolo*," Tyrone replied. "This is a toy that is very popular in China, and people all over the world are trying to find them. We could just have it made, but the Chinese have perfected it, even including whistle windows in the sides." He pointed at the holes at the widest part of each end. "These are the best you can get."

Then, Tyrone fished around inside the crate until he found a sheet of instructions, which he commenced to read, holding it up so that Calyx could see the diagrams. "You twirl the diabolo on the rope like this, you see," he said, motioning toward the picture.

Calyx wound the center of the rope around the area between the two goblet bodies and held the sticks in each hand, clumsily moving them upward and downward to make the diabolo spin. "What is the point?" he asked his uncle.

"It's a toy!" Tyrone replied with a grin. "The point is to entertain yourself with it."

Calyx spun it along the rope a few times, beginning to get the feel of it.

"You can do tricks with it, my boy. This will be all the rage when the children in Teversall see it. I want you to practice, Calyx, so that you can demonstrate it to them."

Now it made sense. With realization dawning Calyx's brow, he studied the instruction sheet, which illustrated ways to fling the diabolo into the air and catch it again on the string. As he became more adept and was able to spin it faster and faster, it began to make a whistling sound. A clerk who had been working in the front of the store smiled brightly as he walked toward them. "That is wonderful!"

Calyx twirled the diabolo, smiling as he attempted to toss it and catch it, and Tyrone chuckled discreetly to the clerk. "If I can't get the boy to play with toys on his own, I know he will do it in order to sell more of them! It's nice to see him acting like a child for a change."

The clerk grinned in agreement. "Of course, he's contemplating physics this entire time, you know."

Indeed, Calyx was so enthralled with working in the shop that, although he did get along well with all the young people in

Teversall, he preferred not to leave himself much time to socialize with them. The shop provided him with much more interesting diversions.

Tyrone taught him about taking special orders, one of the more lucrative areas of the business. They did not necessarily *stock* everything in the world, but they liked to think that they did *sell* everything. If a customer came in looking for a bronze sculpture of an elephant, Tyrone and Calyx were determined to find one. They would ask local craftspeople or write letters until the item was in the store. Sometimes, it took many months, but they would nearly always make it happen. Calyx liked that feeling of empowerment. He had lived his entire life thinking that some things (indeed, most things) were impossible ... even hopeless. But now, he was beginning to disagree.

By the time he was thirteen years old, Calyx came to be considered second-in-charge at Overton's. The adult employees who had worked there for years resented him a little, but they couldn't dislike him. He added something to the whimsical store that gave it more personality, if that were possible.

Tyrone, at that time, allowed Calyx to trade on his behalf when he was not available. This was a significant gesture. He began by letting the boy deal with a coppersmith who brought in several sets of candlesticks. Calyx paid him an amount very close to what Tyrone would have paid him. A woman came in with a beautifully embroidered coverlet. He paid her the correct amount as well. After a while, Tyrone had no reservations whatsoever about leaving Calyx in charge of the operation, and he began to give him a regular salary.

One afternoon when Tyrone was away from the store, an elderly woman walked in carrying a very distinctive set of silverware. She was not familiar with Calyx and asked to speak to Mr. Tyrone Overton, eyeing the other employees suspiciously.

"My uncle is out, but I can help you, madam," Calyx said from behind the counter.

Conveying a hint of shrewdness, the old woman raised an eyebrow at the notion of trading with a youngster like Calyx. She laid the cutlery out on the counter and said, "Solid silver. Amber inlay. Gnome-made."

The first two sentences had been impressive. The third threw him off. "Pardon me? Where were these items made?"

"They were made by gnomes," she said plainly, watching his face with an amused eye. "Get a magnifier. The handiwork should leave no doubt."

He pulled a glass from the drawer below the counter and looked closely at a spoon. It was definitely hammered silver, shaped brilliantly with absolute symmetry and polished to perfection. The handle was adorned by a long teardrop-shaped piece of genuine amber, affixed seamlessly.

He had no idea how to determine whether or not it had been made by gnomes.

"May I ask … *how* you acquired these?"

"I purchased them," she said. "You are not familiar with gnome-made objects? They are rare and extremely valuable."

"I can see that," he said. He had never seen such well-made silverware. He picked up a salad fork and noted how evenly its weight was distributed. He balanced it across the tip of his index finger. If it had been made by humans in a city that he had heard of, pricing them would have been relatively easy, but he didn't want to suggest that price and risk insulting her. She clearly expected him to appreciate that gnome-made items were worth more. Then again, what if she was a fraud, trying to sell them for much more than they were worth?

Finally, Calyx decided to play it safe. "I am sorry. My name is Calyx Overton. I didn't hear your name."

"I am Mrs. Wrigley."

"Mrs. Wrigley, my uncle is just down the street. Would you mind waiting here for just a moment while I get him? I think that he would like to see these items himself."

She looked a bit disappointed, but she smiled. "Of course."

Calyx carried a French parlor chair upholstered in orange velvet to Mrs. Wrigley so that she could wait in comfort, and then dashed through the door, pleased, a moment later, to find that his uncle was still lingering at the coffee shop.

"Uncle Tyrone, I'm sorry to interrupt." Calyx bowed politely at the gentlemen who had been visiting with his uncle. "There is a dealer in the store and I'm not comfortable naming a price."

"Well, this is a first!" Tyrone picked up his hat and bid his friends a good day as he stood to leave with Calyx. "What kind of dealer is this?"

"It's an older woman with a set of amber-inlayed silverware. She says it was made by gnomes. Is she mad?"

"Oh—Mrs. Wrigley?"

"Yes!"

Tyrone patted Calyx on the back as they walked toward the shop. "Calyx, I'm glad you came for me. She is a tough one to trade with, but she always used to bring extraordinary goods. I haven't seen her in years. I didn't even know that she was still alive. Anyway, she is not mad. Or perhaps she is mad, but she is not lying. The silverware is gnomish."

Calyx was utterly intrigued. "There are gnomes? Real gnomes? Where do they live? How does she buy things from them? What else do they make?"

Tyrone laughed. "It is fantastic, isn't it, Calyx? I will tell you what I know later on, although you will be disappointed to find that it's not much. Now, pay close attention while we conduct this transaction."

They entered the store and Tyrone greeted her cordially. "Mrs. Wrigley! It is so nice to see you again."

She stood up and smiled. "Nice to see you as well, Mr. Overton. It was also a pleasure to meet your handsome nephew. Will he be taking over the business one day?"

Tyrone grinned. "Perhaps. He seems to really have a knack for it. Now, you've brought us this gorgeous gnomish collection of cutlery. Let me see it." He stepped behind the counter, picked up the magnifying glass and examined several of the pieces.

Calyx was still stunned that humans traded with gnomes at all. He watched his uncle intently, aware that Mrs. Wrigley was keeping an eye on him.

"I have never seen anything like this," Tyrone declared. "Their expertise is immeasurable, making it terribly hard to price anything. I doubt that there is another set of cutlery in the world exactly like this one."

"Indeed there isn't," the woman shook her head. "You know they never duplicate things like this."

"How about … fifty-five iolos? Will that do?"

She thought about it. "Fifty-five? I was hoping for at least seventy. It was quite an ordeal to get these from them."

Calyx used all the muscles in his face to keep his mouth from bursting with inquiry about *how* she had gotten it from them, but of course he had to stay quiet and watch the transaction. He was already anxious to ask Tyrone a thousand questions about it later on.

"That sounds a little …" Tyrone was apparently going to call her price 'high,' but stop just short of it. "Mrs. Wrigley, I can go to sixty and that is my final bid."

"Sixty." She lifted her face and looked around the room, stopping her eyes at a brown-stained straw bonnet adorned with several rows of thin, dark red ribbons. "If you will throw in that sunbonnet, we have a deal."

Tyrone didn't look surprised. "A deal we shall have." He reached into his own jacket pocket and handed her sixty iolos. Calyx packed the silverware back into the case she had brought it in and Mrs. Wrigley took the bonnet off of its hanger. "I hope it will not be such a long time before we see you again," Tyrone said to her.

"It might be, or it might not be," she said. "I have been far too busy lately to do much trading, but I did take a special liking to this silverware. They are doing wonderful things with amber these days." Then she looked at Calyx. When he met her eyes, she said, "You could trade with them, lad."

"I could?" Calyx doubted that.

She nodded and turned to Tyrone. "He could, Mr. Overton. Believe it."

"How do you know that?" Calyx asked.

"I can just tell. A little bluebird told me. Or maybe it was a little bee."

She left.

# Chapter 9

That evening after dinner, Calyx followed Tyrone into the drawing room. Mr. Overton usually liked to read the paper or a book at this time, but he saw Calyx trailing him with a comically inquisitive glow in his eyes and decided not to bother seeking reading material. There was no fire that evening, as the weather was warming up, but they sat in the chairs nearest the fire anyway, out of habit.

"You have questions," Tyrone detected with a grin.

Calyx sat up in his chair and clasped his hands together, ready to begin asking the questions that he had saved all day long. "Yes. Where do the gnomes live?"

"I'm not certain, but I believe they reside mostly in the wooded areas. I have heard that a large community of them lives in the great pine forest outside of Brudovel."

"Have you ever seen a gnome?"

"No."

"Have you ever tried to?"

"No."

"How large is a gnome?"

"I don't know. I think they are quite miniature."

"Have you done business with gnomes?"

"Only through Mrs. Wrigley."

"How does she do business with them?"

"I imagine that she goes to them and purchases items for one price and then sells them for a higher price elsewhere. She has never given particulars about their transactions."

"Have you asked her for particulars?"

"No." Tyrone chuckled at Calyx's enthusiasm. "My boy, you are going to fall out of that chair. I haven't questioned her because it doesn't matter. It's just business. Gnomes are the finest artisans and craftspeople on the planet and their goods fetch a respectable sum. Do you know how much money I will receive for that silver set she brought in today?"

"How much?"

"One hundred and fifty iolos. Within two weeks, someone will come in and buy it for that price."

"Uncle, don't you want to know what she paid them for it?"

"It doesn't matter," Tyrone repeated.

But it mattered to Calyx. "Do gnomes shop? If she paid them twenty or thirty iolos, what do they do with it?"

"I have no idea," he said. "That is a good question, but is that the last one yet?"

"Oh, no. Uncle Tyrone, she said that I could trade with the gnomes. What do you think she meant by that?"

"I wondered the same thing, Calyx. She has been coming in for many years and I have never heard her say anything like that to anyone. It is my understanding that gnomes are excellent at concealing themselves from humans, and they only associate with certain individuals. Perhaps you are one of those lucky people."

Calyx finally sat back in his chair and gazed absently at the empty fireplace. What would make him one of those preferred people? Why didn't either of them think to ask her to elaborate? What had she meant about the bluebird … or bee?

Blue bee? That had to be a coincidence. Still, he stored it in his memory.

"I want to try," he announced.

"Try?"

"I want to try to trade with them. Uncle, can you imagine having lots of gnome-made items in the shop?"

"That would be something, but I have no information to give you on where to begin trying. Mrs. Wrigley might not appreciate it if we asked her."

"She hinted at it, Uncle! Why would she even say something like that if she didn't want me to do it?"

Tyrone was apprehensive. The forests between the towns were immense, and Calyx was not a seasoned woodsman. He hadn't spent much time at all in the wilderness, and when he had it had been almost exclusively on well-traveled foot paths and in the company of a footman. He was only thirteen years old. "I think it is too great of a risk, Calyx. I'm not that greedy."

"I'm not greedy either," Calyx argued. "I'm very curious, though."

Tyrone's cheeks brightened as he laughed good-naturedly. "There is no doubt about that."

"Uncle Tyrone, please consider it. I'm not afraid. And I would bring my compass and all sorts of safety things."

They both grew quiet. Calyx was letting his uncle think. Tyrone lit a pipe and looked around the room, weighing his fears for Calyx's safety against his inclination to allow the boy to undertake a remarkable mission.

Finally, he answered. "When you are sixteen, I will allow it. You will be older, larger, and wiser. Is that a deal?"

Calyx, whose entire life had been about deals, was disappointed. Three years to a boy feels like thirty to an adult. However, Tyrone looked quite resolute, so Calyx conceded. "It's a deal."

Of course, he went to the library the next day and borrowed every book that looked as if it had content in it about gnomes. He gradually read everything he could find, but the information was often conflicting. The books did not seem to be written by anyone with much first-hand knowledge. Although he was always on the lookout for Mrs. Wrigley, finding her proved nearly impossible. She was an elusive woman, and he had never heard anyone mention of exactly where she lived. Tyrone thought she resided in a remote area outside of town. Someone must know more about her, they figured, but neither of them felt comfortable asking anyone.

Calyx received a letter from his mother every few months. She was going by the name Jane Presser and when Clara gave him her letters, she always referred to her as his Aunt Jane. He hated it, but treasured the letters. During his studies of the gnomes, he received one and took it to his room to read it by the window.

Dear Calyx,

     I hope this letter finds you as well as the last one did. I am so glad to hear that you are an accomplished student and a fine helper to your aunt and uncle Overton, who have been very good to you. It is important to work hard in everything you do.

     Things are fine here. As you know, I have been promoted to Housekeeper and I now have a wonderful room, neither damp nor drafty, and an excellent salary. The duke and duchess treat me very well. I am fortunate. Hallam is a beautiful place. I hope you shall see it one day.

     Please give my best to everyone. I look forward to hearing your updates. As always, I am,


Your loving aunt,

Jane

The letters meant a lot to him. It was a comfort just to know that his mother was still alive and healthy. She sounded happy, too. Some of her letters gave accounts of new employees at the manor that had come from horrible situations in other homes, so he was grateful that she was treated well and paid well.

What he didn't like was the obscure nature of all of the letters. There were many things that she would not say plainly. She seemed too cautious. They had left Rimmolan five years ago and he considered the danger behind them, but she seemed to consider it just as near as it had ever been. He felt sorry for her for that.

He didn't understand why their lives had changed so drastically. He was young when it all happened, and his memory was clouded. He wasn't even sure if he was the same boy who had lived on a farm in Rimmolan—the boy named Charlie Blythe. He didn't feel like he knew anything about farming. Or straw plaiting.

Yes, he remembered the straw plaiting. The truth was that he could still do it with his eyes closed if he had to. He had learned it right along with walking and talking. He had learned it before he could write his own name. He had learned it before he could tie his shoes. Yet she never mentioned it. Sometimes he longed to buy some lengths of straw, split them, and braid a bundle just to feel like Charlie Blythe again for an hour.

He wondered if she ever had the same thoughts, but he couldn't ask.

They continued to correspond, and Clara wrote to Sigrid often, as well. It was awkward for Clara. She was Calyx's new mother, by most accounts, and she couldn't have loved him more if he were her own son. He had their father's eyes. Her eyes. Blythe eyes. She had twelve other nieces and nephews, but he was by far the most promising of them all, and she was glad that she and Tyrone were able to raise him. She felt selfish about it sometimes, but glad.

# Chapter 10

It took a long time, but eventually Calyx did turn sixteen. The Overtons were in the position to send him to the university, and they had planned on doing so for some time, but Calyx didn't want them to spend the money. He reasoned that he had no problem finding plenty of intellectual diversions in business and in life.

Mrs. Wrigley had come in to Overton's Curios a few more times, but she only spoke cryptically when Calyx asked about the gnomes. He didn't understand it. Why had she hinted about him dealing with them directly if she had no intention of giving him any guidance about how to do so? Was she trying to tell him something else?

Many of the young ladies in town had their eye on the handsome, young, up-and-coming businessman, and all of their mothers considered him entirely suitor material. Tyrone and Clara were not necessarily aristocratic, as they did earn a living from trade (unlike the gentlemen and ladies who simply lived off of their inheritances), but the Overtons were well respected, well dressed, well connected, and well apportioned financially, and Calyx was intelligent, charming, and confident.

These maidens' families began to hobnob with the Overtons excessively, inviting them to dinner so often that Clara wondered how she would ever return all the invitations. She and Tyrone found it amusing nonetheless, and they obliged. It was awkward for Calyx. Most of the young ladies seemed dull and ignorant to him, and that was exacerbated by the fact that dullness and ignorance were often touted as desirable female virtues and, therefore, exaggerated in his presence.

Tyrone saw this and hoped that Calyx would continue to handle it well, still convinced that a university setting would have been better for the boy. "It's fortunate that he is a boy," he joked to Clara one day. "He will not have to turn down proposals, anyway."

Clara laughed. "He's only sixteen. He has all the time in the world to find a wife. I am not sure that any of the Teversall young ladies thus far, as lovely as some of them are, have been nearly sharp enough to interest him." But she did hope that Calyx would marry one day and continue her brother's bloodline. She still missed Charles dearly.

As Tyrone expected, Calyx had not forgotten about their deal. A few weeks after his sixteenth birthday, the boy announced, "Uncle, I'm ready to try my hand at trading with gnomes. I assume that you still approve?"

Tyrone nodded with a grin. "I have no choice, do I, my boy? Do you have a plan? Do you know where to go, how to get there, and when to do it?"

"I know where the forest is. I can take a horse, with your permission. And the sooner, the better."

"Take the grey Barb," Tyrone said, referring to the Spanish horse that Calyx preferred to ride. "And I think it would be wise to take someone along."

"I believe that would destroy my chances," Calyx said. "Uncle, if I leave at sun-up, I can get there by midday and be home before dark. Don't you think so?"

Tyrone calculated. "Six hours each way? Perhaps." Then, the apprehension returned. "Why are you so determined to do this, Calyx? I hope not just to make me richer."

"Only partly," Calyx grinned. "I think the biggest reason, though, is because I can. It seems a travesty not to do something when you can."

That settled it. Tyrone approved. "You are very exceptional, Calyx. I'm proud of you. I give you leave to go any day you choose."

Two days later, before dawn, Calyx left the house on the grey Barb named Jasper. He took his silver compass, his gold Geneva pocket watch, a small utility knife, two canteens of water, a bag of dried fruit, bread, boiled eggs, and plenty of money.

He was riding toward Brudovel, a town he had heard much about, but had never seen. If he had time to go even further, he would go into town and see it for himself. It was much different from Teversall in some interesting ways.

Teversall was part of the kingdom of Wulkelin, the seat of which was twenty-five miles to the north. Citizens of Teversall were subjects of the king in Wulkelin and paid their dues to the crown, but did not have much else to do with it, other than take comfort in the protection that was guaranteed to all parts of the kingdom. Most of the residents of Teversall were fair, even-tempered, and community-minded, each playing an active role in the bustling little town. As a result, very few residents were poor.

Brudovel was as large as Teversall, but more secluded in nature. It was ruled by a royal family of its own and most of the people who lived there were of the middle or lower class. Perhaps they had to pay more to the crown, or perhaps the people in Teversall got away with paying less to theirs. Whatever the case, this was only one distinction.

He had heard that the citizens of Brudovel themselves were peculiar. Each underwent a bizarre personality change of some sort at the age of ten, and some believed that the fairies of Brudovel were responsible. Most laughed at the notion of fairies existing at all. Calyx didn't know what to believe, or why that would happen, but as he rode closer to that place, he vowed to himself to go there one day and see it for himself.

Not today, however. He had business to conduct and he had to return home before dark.

He left Teversall and followed the rough road beyond the remote farm areas, around a series of green, sparsely-wooded hills, and along the edge of a forest filled with various hardwoods, stopping several times to stretch his legs and water Jasper. Solitary trips were tiring for Calyx, as he liked to talk, but he amused himself by identifying rarely-seen plants along the way.

Finally, the forest began to creep up on both sides and the road felt darker, even though the day in general was at its brightest. When he could see no clearing in his view in any direction and all of the trees were extraordinarily tall and stately-standing pines, he knew he had arrived at the great pine forest. *How long should I continue?* he wondered. *Should I look for a path leading into the forest?* And then he just stopped.

There might not be a path. Why would there be? People never went into this forest. It was shadowy and some considered it haunted … or at least enchanted. He felt a little foolish. He considered walking into it, saying, "Here, gnomy, gnomy!" He tried to imagine what Mrs. Wrigley did when she arrived.

The trees were so imposing that very few other plants grew on the ground. He was surprised at how clear the spaces were between the trees, and he beckoned Jasper to enter the forest with him. There was plenty of room for a horse.

He held his compass in his hand. He would need it, as it was one o'clock and the sun was quite near the center of the sky. He decided to continue on a straight eastern path so that he could just exit by going west.

Jasper walked slowly, unfazed by the deep silence. After about five minutes, both of them turned their heads toward a rustle that came from a tree bough to their right. They saw nothing and continued.

A few minutes more and suddenly, a black-billed magpie squawked and swooped down from above, landing on a branch nearby. Its long tail stabilized the weight of a tiny, red-capped man who was sitting on the bird's back. The small, red conical hat on the man's head was the only bit of color in the entire forest that did not blend with the trees.

Calyx stopped Jasper. His heart pounded as he hopped off the horse and stared at the little man, who confidently climbed off the magpie's back and stood on the branch, steadying himself with his hand on a smaller limb. "Greetings and welcome," he said to Calyx.

It was almost exactly the way he had pictured a gnome to look. White beard, pointed hat, and simple clothing with round, rosy cheeks and nose. But he had imagined gnomes to be small people. This man was no taller than the bird he had ridden in on.

"Thank you," Calyx replied, trying to breathe slowly. "I am Calyx Overton, of Teversall. My uncle owns a curio shop."

"Ah," the gnome replied. "It is nice to meet you, Mister Overton. My name is Ghab. A friend who saw you enter the forest a little while ago just called me to greet you. I am the leader of the society. They call me King Ghab."

A gnome king! Calyx felt exceptionally fortunate. "It is a pleasure to meet you, King Ghab. Very much a pleasure."

Ghab looked at Calyx for a moment and Calyx wondered why he was nodding. Then Calyx said, "I have come to ask for a trade."

"A trade. Well, what are you looking for?"

This looked promising. He decided to throw in a referral to help the process along. "A Mrs. Wrigley comes into our shop from time to time with items that your … that the gnome society has made. They sell very well. I am especially interested in your hammered metal home goods, but I would like to see anything. Really, sir, the finest things in the world come from your people."

Were they people?

King Ghab was pleased. "Absolutely," he said. He called Jasper to him with a click and a hand gesture. The horse went to the little king and bent its head down; Ghab grabbed a hold of its mane and climbed to the top of its head. Calyx watched, his mouth agape. Then Ghab said, "Hop on, Mister Overton."

As instructed, Calyx mounted Jasper and took the reins, but Ghab led the horse. Calyx held the reins loosely and watched in awe as the gnome directed Jasper toward the left and then the right. *What a relief that I brought the compass,* he thought.

Soon, they reached a spot that, at first glance, looked no different from the rest of the forest. Ghab said something to Jasper. The horse bent its head again and let the king off onto another tree, from which he scrambled to the earthen floor and instructed Calyx to follow him.

Hidden among many other pines stood one tree with a trunk so wide, its stump could have served as a dance floor. King Ghab led Calyx behind it, where a pair of grey foxes who guarded the tree greeted him fondly. He patted them each on their bristly heads, kicked the bottom of the tree, and the bark opened, revealing a room inside the trunk. Then, he motioned for Calyx to follow him inside.

# Chapter 11

Within the tree two other gnomes greeted Ghab, who introduced them as Cobbkin and Migmor, a brother and sister who had been working on a pair of pewter candlesticks when their guest arrived. They greeted Calyx jovially as he ducked through the door.

They motioned for him to sit in a human-sized chair by the doorway. Too tall to stand upright in the room, he gladly took a seat. "What would Mister Overton like to buy?" Cobbkin asked Ghab.

Ghab turned to Calyx. "Look over our inventory, Mister Overton. We can settle on an agreement for anything in this room."

Calyx scanned the many low, wooden tables. There were a great deal of household items that would sell in an instant at Overton's Curios. Copper wall sconces, silver serving platters, crystal lamps, elaborate window treatments, and fine ceramic dishes filled the room. He wanted all of it.

He decided to choose one piece to start with, just to get an idea of what they charged. He pointed at a silver pepper mill with an ornamental design that resembled woven water reeds carved along the base and lid. The sides were pierced into a vine-like pattern and behind the silver the pot was elegantly lined in smooth, dark green crystal. Cobbkin carried it to Calyx, who noted that it was unusually heavy and the lid turned easily. "Remarkable," he commented, admiring it from all sides and noting the bottom, engraved only with the letters T and B. "How much would you like for this?"

The gnomes looked at each other.

Perhaps he should have made an outright offer. He came up with one. "Thirty iolos?"

King Ghab asked him, "Is this the only item you would like to purchase?"

"No, sir," Calyx replied. "I am sure there are many more, if I can afford them."

"You can afford anything here," Ghab told him. "But we do not trade for human currency. Iolos are of no use to us, unless we were to melt them down and make something of the metal."

Just as he had wondered. "I am sorry," he said. "I did not bring any gold with me. I only have iolos."

"We do not trade for gold either," King Ghab added.

That was odd. "Well, I think I must pose the question to you, then," Calyx replied. "What would you like for this splendid pepper pot?"

Ghab scratched his head and began to explain. "Mister Overton, this depends on what you wish to buy. Select your items and then we will make an agreement."

Rather perturbed that this six-inch-tall man was making him feel like a fool, Calyx sighed and looked around. He selected a silver mirror bordered with a crystal grapevine design, a blue glass soda siphon, a silver ribbed snuff box, and a pair of cut crystal candlesticks. Cobbkin and Migmor set the items on the low table in front of Calyx as he chose them. Calyx was not sure how he could possibly carry it all back to Teversall safely, but it seemed like a good assortment for his first gnomish trade.

"Very good eye," King Ghab remarked.

"How do I pay for them, sir?" Calyx asked.

Ghab eyed the merchandise and his lips moved silently as he calculated their value. He closed his eyes and thought for a moment and then said, "Maps. Please bring us maps of at least twenty different countries. They must be detailed, labeled, and purchased from a mapmaker. Will that be possible?"

"Maps?"

"Yes. All of our maps are quite outdated."

Calyx couldn't help it. He burst out laughing. He tried to cover his mouth and stop laughing, as the others were staring at him as if he were laughing at their grandmother's wake, but he had never in his life been in such a hilarious situation.

"Mister Overton, do we have a deal?"

Calyx did some quick math and found the price of twenty maps to be almost nothing compared to the amount of money that a few wealthy patrons would pay for the gnome-made items on the table before him. Even if the news stand in Teversall didn't have maps of twenty different countries, he could order some and have them within a few weeks.

"It is a deal," Calyx nodded, finally containing his laughter into a slight grin. "It might take me two or three weeks, but I will get them to you."

King Ghab smiled and shook his hand. "Excellent. Return with the maps and we shall give you the items at that time."

Calyx's face dropped. He had hoped to leave the forest with commodities in his hands, but it was fair. King Ghab recognized his disenchantment and handed him the pepper pot.

"You may take this today, as assurance of our good faith. I am very glad that you came here, Mister Overton. There are many things that we want."

"Thank you very much, King Ghab," he said. It was strange calling him king, as he wore no crown and seemed rather plain and forbearing. "I will bring the maps as soon as I possibly can."

Calyx thanked the others and Ghab accompanied him out of the tree room. The hospitable gnome king hopped back onto Jasper's head and escorted them back to the edge of the woods near the road.

Calyx checked his Geneva pocket watch. It was only two o'clock. He wondered if he could spare an hour or so to see those infamously peculiar, fairy-cursed people in Brudovel, but decided against it.

There would be time another day and, as it was, he would just barely make it back to Teversall by dark. He was anxious to show his uncle the pepper pot, and could hardly wait to visit the news stand first thing in the morning.

# Chapter 12

Calyx scoured the Teversall marketplace the next morning, unable to find more than three detailed country maps. He carried them into Overton's Curios, where his uncle stood behind the counter.

The pepper pot was displayed beside the register. Tyrone priced it at eighty-five iolos, quite high for something as practical as a pepper pot. The craftsmanship was indisputable, however. Tyrone knew that someone would come in and consider it well worth the price. Considering the effort it took for Calyx to ride so far, and the courage it took for him to obtain it, he didn't feel guilty. All of that must be worth something.

Tyrone and Calyx had decided the night before that they would not reveal to anyone how they had gotten the item. Their dealings with the gnomes must remain a secret. Nobody would ask, as he had sold gnome items for years and it was generally understood that dealers brought the merchandise into the store. It wasn't likely that anyone would suspect Calyx of being the dealer.

Keeping their business matters private was not Calyx's main concern, however. He didn't wish to embolden the people of the town to invade the pine forest in search of gnomish goods. Although he was quite sure that the gnomes could defend themselves, especially with all of the forest animals protecting them, Calyx couldn't bear the thought of humans intruding on the kind little creatures and disrupting their lives.

As he approached his uncle at the register, Calyx tucked the three maps into a shelf beneath the counter and said with regret, "Only three."

"I will send to London," Tyrone replied, not at all surprised. "I'll get as many as I can, in case they ask for more in the future. Whatever they don't need, we can just put on the back rack."

Calyx grinned. He knew that Tyrone's *we can sell it* attitude was the key to his success. Sometimes, it was downright humorous. A letter went out to London that day; Calyx hoped that Tyrone would dispatch him to go personally, but that didn't happen this time. Two weeks later, Calyx was present to receive the package as it arrived. Dozens of high quality, neatly rolled maps were inside, representing forty-two different countries. With the three maps he already had, he knew that he would be able to go back to the forest and choose twice as many items as he had originally selected. This time, he took the carriage and two horses.

Along the way, he passed a neat little thatched-roofed farmhouse with a large wheat field at one side and a barn with a rolling horse pasture at the other. A man in his twenties, wearing a pair of overalls and a roughly-hewn derby hat, was carrying a pail of water into the barn.

Calyx didn't remember much about his father. Occasionally, he could picture Charles Senior's face through the eyes of a three-year-old, but that was it. He imagined that his father's voice was similar to Tyrone's, and that his father would have joked around with him the way his uncle did, but there were so many contrasts. His father knew nothing of life in a town, or of trade. Indeed, Sigrid had always handled their business dealings.

It saddened him, sometimes, being on a path so different from his father's. Had Charles not died, Calyx would know a great deal more about fence-mending and roof-thatching than bartering and procuring popular items, but he wondered if Charles would have preferred the more privileged life if that had ever been an option to him.

*I'm fortunate, and I need to appreciate the good things that have happened,* Calyx decided resolutely. *I think my father would be pleased to see me becoming a tradesman; I am good at it. And to deal with gnomes is even better.*

Calyx couldn't recall much about his father's likes and dislikes, but he comforted himself with the notion that any man who could build all the things that Charles had built would undoubtedly be impressed by the craftsmanship of the gnomes. He waved as the man emerged from the barn with an empty pail and continued onward.

Of course, he couldn't easily navigate the carriage through the wilderness, so when Calyx reached the pine forest, he stopped at the edge, pulled the enormous sack of maps from the bed of the carriage and took a few steps into the woodland. He had been considering the safety of the horses throughout the ride and now wished that he could have taken a trusted footman or some companion with him. Even their bulldog could have ridden along and protected the horses.

After just a few minutes of standing around, contemplating what to do, a very large brown bear approached, making enough of a rustling sound from a distance to give the boy plenty of warning. Calyx began to dash toward the carriage, but was stopped by a small but commanding voice that said, "It is all right, Mister Overton. I heard that you had a cart. Arctos will hide right here and watch the horses."

This made Calyx extremely nervous. He didn't know much about bears, but leaving one alone with two horses seemed like a terrible idea. The bear slumped down cozily and nestled behind a tree, facing the horses, who didn't seem to notice the bear.

*Well, this is an enchanted forest,* Calyx reasoned.

Rabbits, he progressively learned, were the gnomes' preferred mode of ground transportation. They were just the right size: the proportion being similar to that of a human on a horse. A brown hare appeared from somewhere (it was difficult to tell in this forest, as they, like the other animals, were camouflaged perfectly), waited for King Ghab to climb onto its back, and hopped alongside Calyx toward what he began to refer to mentally as the Trading Tree.

It didn't seem as far this time, and Calyx wondered if the gnomes somehow moved trees around, or if there were, in fact, several impossibly-wide pines in this forest. Perhaps they frequently relocated their inventory from tree to tree to keep it safe. He wanted to ask, but they were already there, and he had business to do.

All of the items that they had been holding for him were packed in a wooden box, each piece securely padded with broad, soft fern leaves. The box sat beside the door as if it were expecting him. "You have brought us the maps?" Ghab asked.

"Yes, sir. In fact, I brought you forty-five maps in hopes that you would allow me to purchase additional items today."

"Lovely!" King Ghab exclaimed. "I shall look them over. In the meantime, please start choosing more things and I will tell you when to stop."

That was intimidating. Calyx would have preferred to have some idea of how many items he could choose, but Ghab seemed resolute in his system of trading and Calyx had no intention of complaining. He was getting outrageously good prices for everything so far.

He took a few toys this time: a ceramic-faced doll in a flouncy white lace dress, a wonderful hand-painted papier-mâché jack-in-the-box, and a hand-carved pine rocking horse. He looked at Ghab, wondering how much credit he still had available. Ghab did not stop him, so he chose an exquisite sterling teapot with a faceted swan-necked spout and a chased scrolling leaf decoration on each side. He stopped for a moment to admire that teapot before continuing. The work the gnomes did was amazing.

Finally, he noticed some jewelry far across the room. It was rather dark on that side of the Trading Tree and he hadn't yet asked to examine any of it, but Cobbkin was right beside the table. "May I see some of the jewelry?" Calyx asked.

Cobbkin nodded agreeably and carried a tray across the room, setting it on the table. Instantly, Calyx wished he hadn't chosen anything else. His mouth hung open as he studied the jewels before him. The thick, bark-covered door completely closed out the sun and the candle lamps only offered the room a soft glow, but somehow, each gem still sparkled brightly, as if it possessed its own source of energy.

"How do they glisten like this?" he asked, not wanting to touch the colorful flickering stones. "What type of gems *are* these?"

"Common," Cobbkin replied, grinning at Ghab. "All gems are common."

King Ghab clarified. "It's in the faceting, Mister Overton. Pick up one of the pieces to see how it is cut."

He lifted a green-jeweled ring and held it up, a few inches from his eyes. Turning it, he saw the intricate slices between each edge. He had never seen a gemstone shine like that. Could the way a stone was faceted really make such an enormous difference? "Amazing," he said. "Amazing!"

"It takes a great deal of understanding and skill to cut a stone like that, but we think the result is worth it," Ghab said with pride. "Cobbkin is the best gem-cutter of them all."

Cobbkin blushed through his already rosy smile, but didn't deny it.

Calyx tried to imagine how they did it. The gem had no table at all, not a pointed top. It was covered with infinitesimal, perfectly symmetrical angles, giving it a generally globular shape. This jewelry would, without the smallest doubt, fetch a colossal price.

"May I take a piece of jewelry with me?" he asked, hoping that they wouldn't laugh.

They didn't, but Ghab did draw up a very serious expression. "Mister Overton, I see that you find those objects to be most valuable."

"Oh, indeed!"

"What is it about that ring that is of value?"

Calyx looked at it, scrambling mentally to determine the answer that Ghab would like to hear. "It's the clear, brilliantly-colored stone, the expertly molded gold setting, and the … incredibly extraordinary way that the stone is cut."

"Would you like it as much if the stone were just a rough chunk of crystal?"

"Not nearly."

"Would you like it as much if the setting were uneven, dull pewter?"

"No, but I would still find the stone wonderful."

"Would you like it as much if the stone were blue? Or red?"

"I believe so."

"What, then, truly makes it valuable to you … and to your customers?"

"The faceting, sir."

"Is that not interesting, Mister Overton?"

"It is."

Calyx considered it. The work that had gone into making the stone so brilliant determined its entire value. "And that is the way many things are."

King Ghab and Cobbkin both nodded, and Ghab said, "Humans need to learn that, but I fear they never will. You, as a businessman and a person who will one day be of great influence to many humans, would do well to understand it completely while you are still young. As humans age, they think they become wiser, but that rarely occurs."

Calyx smiled archly to hear such an impetuous statement about the contrast between the old and the young. He wondered how old these gnomes were. He wondered why King Ghab thought that he would one day be influential to many people.

Cobbkin seemed to take a silent cue from Ghab. He took a deep breath, as if to begin a new chapter of the conversation. "Mister Overton, we are in the process of building a large quantity of silver flutes for our orchestra. Please tell me ... how is a flute like the Queen of Brudovel?"

Calyx glanced at him, and then at Ghab, hoping that one of them would add something sensible to that question, but they only watched his face with anticipation. "Is this a riddle?"

"It is," Cobbkin replied, nodding.

Calyx thought. And thought. He wasn't sure how clever these gnomes were regarding riddles. *They both wear silver?* That was too dull. *They both live in Brudovel now?* Too obvious, given what he was just told. *Why do they expect me to answer this silly question?*

But they both knew what kind of a human Calyx was. He had come all the way to the forest just to trade with them. He had brought them twice the number of maps they required. They understood a little bit about his background. They knew he would think until he found the correct answer to the riddle … not in spite of it being a difficult thing to do, but because it was difficult.

He tried to pull up what he knew about the Queen of Brudovel, which was not much. Her husband was dead. She had two or three children, all cursed in strange ways by the fairies of Brudovel. He had heard that the people of the town were unclear about which child would inherit the throne.

The queen needed an heir. A flute needed air. Could that be the solution? He tried it, with a hint of modest uncertainty in his voice. "Both are in need of a little *heir*?"

Cobbkin applauded merrily. "Oh, Mister Overton, you do not disappoint. Well done, sir. Very well done." Ghab grinned at the clever human admirably.

Calyx smiled politely, waiting to hear if he could take the ring with him.

Cobbkin hopped onto the table and closed the ring into its box. "I knew you were the correct one," he said, still beaming.

*It really wasn't that tricky,* Calyx thought, almost wishing that they would ask him another one, just for the challenge. "The correct one?" he inquired. "What do you mean, sir?"

Now, Ghab drew a deep breath. "Mister Overton, Cobbkin will teach you his skill, if you promise never to tell anyone how you learned it."

"His skill? Cutting gems?"

They both nodded. Cobbkin said, "Take the ring today. It is worth far more than all the maps, only because of the way it is faceted. I want you to take it and consider that paradox for one week. When you return, I will show you how to take a piece of rock, cast off by the earth itself, and make it into something precious and valuable."

Calyx was jubilant. "Thank you, sir! I do appreciate it very, very much. And I am looking forward to thinking about that, as I have a bit of experience with that sort of theme myself."

"We are aware of that," King Ghab replied with a warm smile.

Arctos the brown bear scampered away unassumingly as Calyx loaded the back of the carriage with his newly-acquired goods. He tucked the ring, in its wooden box, safely into his inner jacket pocket. King Ghab wished him well and Calyx promised exuberantly to return in seven days, completely forgetting to ask what he could bring to them in exchange for more of their goods.

This interesting business project had just become a rather exciting journey.

# Chapter 13

The dryads in the forest of Rimmolan were nothing like the fairies of Brudovel. Although they were permitted to interfere with humans of their tones, rarely did they do it. They knew that there was danger in it and, moreover, they weren't very interested in the humans.

When the others heard that Thea had turned into a bee and stung young Charlie Blythe, they were quite outraged. Although her intent had been only to give him extra strength during wearisome experiences, he would inevitably have a small amount of fairy power beyond that. If he realized that, he could channel it. A dryad never took such chances.

She wished she hadn't told anyone. For months, some of the others scowled at her and turned up their noses when they passed her tree. It was unpleasant, but none of it made her regret what she had done. Even when Calyx was a toddler, she saw how bright and genuinely good he was.

Still, she never let her guard down. The Borgh elf who had helped the Blythes grow their wheat would never forget. She was beginning to feel vexed by it more than ever, and she felt responsible for keeping him away from Calyx.

The elf known as Fenbeck was in Stratskon. Upon sensing this, she felt the need to go there.

Off she flew, disguised as a rock thrush, and arrived in two hours. She sailed over the quaint, remote town of Stratskon, where everything was painted glistening white, yet she did not feel the presence of any sort of fairy living in the land. She used her instinct, something of which fairies possess a great quantity and often use incorrectly, and found the petulant Borgh elf behind a feed store, bitterly writing on a small tablet.

There was no mistaking him for any other sort of elf. He was richly garbed in new satin breeches with silk hose. His fine linen shirt was topped with a bright tangerine overcoat embroidered with zigzags in red and yellow and a green lace-edged tie. This was no modest working elf.

She quietly stopped at a tree overhead and watched him, honing in to get a glimpse of what he was writing. *Sir Geoffrey Prothero.* He was smiling, almost triumphantly. Then, he wrote, *Sigrid Blythe = future Jane Prothero.*

Thea panicked for a second. He was in Stratskon researching Calyx's mother. Was Sigrid here? She had to find Sir Geoffrey Prothero.

Off she flew, examining the countryside from above several stately manors. One of them seemed right, so there she descended. She did not find Sir Geoffrey, but as she peeked into each window on the upper floor, she suddenly spotted Sigrid Blythe herself, brushing her long, flaxen hair before a vast looking glass. The window just two rooms away was open.

Without giving a thought to how foolish a bird would have to be to fly into a human home, Thea courageously stopped on that windowsill and scooted through, navigating her way into Sigrid's room. There, she paused. The lady did not notice her.

Should she?

Thea perched herself atop the crown molding above the door, completely frazzled. She had to warn her, but there was no trouble-free way to do it. She chose the least horrifying way. She turned into something similar to a human.

In a gown the color of the sky on a clear, sunny day, she stood at the doorway and knocked softly, not wishing to startle the lady who sat in the chair with her back to the door. Sigrid heard the knock and glanced into the mirror, setting the brush on the vanity. She stood and smiled oddly.

Thea spoke quickly. "I must have a word with you, Mrs. ... May I close the door?"

"Who are you?" Sigrid asked with increasing alarm.

Thea closed the door. "Sigrid Blythe?"

A soft huff came from Sigrid's stunned mouth. She had not heard her real name in years. "I am not," she said. "You are mistaken. Please leave."

"Mrs. Blythe, do not be afraid of me. I am vexed to do this myself, but I must warn you about something. It is extremely urgent. It is about your son, Charles. Calyx Overton."

Sigrid covered half her face with her hand, unable to decide whether to scream or cry, but realizing that she must listen. The woman knew too much.

Thea continued, "The Borgh elf known as Fenbeck is looking for you. He is here in Stratskon. I believe that he is trying to find Calyx. I cannot leave the forest for too long ..."

"The forest? Who are you?" Sigrid tried to maintain some composure, but this overwhelmed her. Tears began to stream down her cheeks.

Thea sighed. *Why did I mention the forest?*

"What does he want with ... him?" Sigrid asked desperately, still afraid to say the name of her own son. "And why?"

Thea, not wanting to continue to frighten the poor woman by saying her name, could not think of a reasonable lie that would relay the information that Sigrid needed. Dryads were natural story tellers, but they were terrible liars. She studied Sigrid's face for a long while and decided that she would deliver the truth. "I shall tell you."

Sigrid gathered as much composure as she could as she locked the door and sat at her vanity. Thea sat on a chair nearby and began.

"There is a land sixty miles from here known as Borgh. You have never heard of it because humans no longer live there. They did at one time. Briefly.

"Long ago, it was all wilderness. There was a river, many forest animals, and a large population of beavers, who shaped the streams with a series of dams and lived in sturdy lodges all along the banks. It was quiet and peaceful.

"A society of fairies lives in the nearby forest. They lived as the dryads do, in quietude and in pleasing seclusion. They had never seen humans before." She watched Sigrid's face for a few seconds, allowing her to absorb the introduction of fairies into the story. Then, she resumed.

"Very abruptly, a group of humans discovered the land and liked it. They built homes, hunted in the forest, fished in the streams, and chopped down the beavers' beloved rowan and willow trees for firewood. More humans came, and more. They destroyed the beavers' primary dam and then many of their secondary dams. They shot some of the beavers and made clothing out of their fur. They attacked their lodges.

"The fairies, who view human life and animal life as equally valuable, were horrified. They had no pity for these humans, but, of course, were not morally capable of harming them. They could send them to another place, but more humans would come.

Their hearts ached for the beavers, which were now hiding by day and scrambling to find food and shelter by night. One fairy suggested cursing the humans somehow, but they could not think of a good spell that would be generally considered benevolent.

"Finally, another suggested that they cast a spell on the beavers instead, making them equal to the humans. They could turn them into wolves or bears, perhaps. After much discussion, the fairies decided that the humans, with their weapons and ingenuity, were likely to drive out even the mightiest of animals. They finally settled on turning the beavers into elves.

"Elves are kind to nature, but far more intelligent than humans. They have some powers and are good at manipulating, but they usually are not excessively greedy or ruthless. These elves, unfortunately, were the exception.

"With a vague memory of their lives as beavers and an enormous resentment for the invading human, the elves relentlessly sabotaged everything the humans did. They destroyed their crops. They let loose their livestock. Eventually, they resorted to burning down their houses. The humans tried to fight back, but the elves were always several steps ahead of them. Frightened and exhausted, the humans ultimately retreated, leaving the land of Borgh with little more than they had originally brought to it … leaving the nasty little elves.

"There is a legend about them around that area, and humans do not dare to venture to Borgh, but I do not think that many of those elves still live there. With nobody to manipulate and nothing to achieve, most of them left. They have earned a great deal of money, as they are unbelievably proficient at everything they do. Unlike those nocturnal beavers, they can work just as hard during the day as at night. I have heard that one Borgh elf is equal in strength and aptitude to a crew of one hundred humans in just about any task that is set before them. I believe that you have seen evidence of that."

"Yes," Sigrid acknowledged serenely. As bizarre as it all was, for the first time, it was beginning to make some sense. "That man is a Borgh elf?"

Thea nodded. "He is. Now, I have heard that the Borgh elves have developed the ability to force certain humans to join their society and become Borgh elves as well. I am not sure if it has ever happened, but since Calyx has some fairy power in him, the elf, I believe, has identified him as one that can be transformed."

"Fairy power! What?" Sigrid sat up in her seat, feeling hopeless and incredulous.

Thea cringed, wishing that she hadn't mentioned that. "Yes, Sigrid. Your son has some fairy power. He doesn't know it, but the elf does."

"How does the elf know? How do you know? Who are you and what is fairy power?"

"I don't want to burden you with too much," Thea said with a kind smile, feeling that the complete story would over-whelm this woman beyond sanity. "Please trust me. I must leave you, but warn Calyx immediately. He is capable. He must remember that he is in hiding for a reason."

Sigrid was not sure. It had been so long since any of the past was mentioned that she considered it possible for him to have forgotten everything. But she could do nothing less than to trust this strange visitor in the sky blue gown. "I will," she said. "Thank you."

Thea quickly and cautiously left the room, closing the door behind her before Sigrid had time to accompany her. Sigrid made it to the door and opened it just in time to catch a glimpse of a small blue thrush darting down the hallway and into a vacant guest room. She rushed toward it and entered the room as it departed through an open window. Sigrid watched the bird fly from the building and across the sky, and she followed it with her stunned yet weary eyes until it disappeared.

Sigrid felt nauseated. As kind as it had been for the Duke of Hallam to orchestrate her marriage to one of his influential friends, the abrupt lifestyle adjustment already overwhelmed her.

Now there was this.

Regardless, nothing mattered except getting a message to Calyx, and Sigrid began to pen one immediately, vexed that she must add this enigmatic warning to a bit of rather urgent news about her future. This would be quite a troubling letter for the good young man to receive.

# Chapter 14

Dear Calyx,

     I am writing to inform you of a decision that I have made. It would be best to announce it to all of you in person, but unfortunately that does not appear to be possible.

     By the time you receive this letter I will be married to Sir Geoffrey Prothero, a landowner in Stratskon. I am currently staying in town at one of his country residences until our wedding day. I am, therefore, no longer in Hallam. I will write again as soon as I am settled. I apologize for the brevity of this letter and the abruptness of the news.

     Martha visited last week in her new azure silk gown. She said that the undersized buttons were here in Stratskon, but did not suit my wardrobe, so they are en route to Teversall to Clara Overton. Please let them know so that you all can be expecting the arrival.

     Your aunt Clara tells me that your contributions to the family business have been very beneficial. I am, as always, proud to call myself,

     Your loving aunt,

     Jane

Calyx, who was drinking his morning tea in the parlor, set the cup on the saucer and reread the entire letter. It was entirely odd. She was going to marry a man whom he had never heard of. Indeed, the wedding had probably already taken place. He wondered whether she had become Mrs. Prothero or if she had a different title. His mother had been working at the duke's manor for eight years and had never mentioned this man. How could she marry him and move to Stratskon without telling any of them about it sooner?

Calyx tried to make sense of it. *Does Sir Geoffrey even know that she had a son? Will I ever be welcomed at their house? How could she?*

At the same time, he was glad that she would no longer be a housekeeper. Now she would have her very own staff. What a sudden and extraordinary shift in circumstances! He collected his senses, comforted in knowing that the Overtons would not do anything quite so unexpected. He didn't need a mother anymore. He could get along without anyone, at this age.

Calyx and Sigrid didn't mutually know a woman named Martha. When he read that, he knew that what followed was going to be nonsense. Why would Calyx care about some unknown lady's blue silk gown, or the buttons that were too small for it? Clearly, Sigrid was trying to tell him something else, but he would have to wait until the package arrived from Hallam to understand any of it.

The new gnomish items procured by Calyx on his last trip to the forest created an enormous stir throughout Teversall. A few people trickled into the store on the first morning to have a look. They told others about it and those people made a point to stop by. That afternoon, the shop was crowded with people of all ages and financial circumstances. The shop had stocked gnome-made goods for years, but usually only one item at a time. Now, gnome-made objects comprised the entire front of the store, and Tyrone directed one of his salespeople to do nothing but stay in that area and watch the highly-priced inventory all day long, just in case one of the hundreds of shoppers felt tempted to walk out with something without paying.

By the end of day three, all of the items had been sold at full price. One man who had no cash with him at the store even offered to pay more for the tea pot just so Mr. Overton would hold it for him. Of course, Tyrone only charged him the tagged price, and the man returned with his payment within ten minutes.

In short, Overton's made a higher profit in three days with those few items than it usually made in two weeks without them. Although the majority of the spectators couldn't afford any of the gnomish items that they had come to see, most of them consequently purchased some other thing before leaving, which further increased Tyrone's overall sales.

Naturally, Tyrone was pleased and he wanted the attraction to continue, but they could not know what other items the gnomes would request. A new supply would require two trips to the forest. He gave Calyx a list of the sort of items that he would like him to obtain and, as promised, the boy rode back to the forest the following week, this time with only Jasper.

Calyx now looked forward to the solitary trip to the pine forest. A sociable young man by nature, he enjoyed spending a great deal of time talking to people at the shop, on the street, and at home, but he had grown to value this quiet journey. When he was on a long ride toward Brudovel, nothing was expected of him. He had no questions to answer; no people to take care of. It was his time to think.

During that particular week, he had many things on his mind and the most pressing of them were not very pleasant. Tyrone and Clara were equally bewildered about his mother's marriage, though also extremely happy for her. They even suggested taking a trip to Stratskon at some point in the future to see her and meet her new husband. It was an awkward notion, as none of them knew if Sir Geoffrey was aware that any of them existed.

Calyx assumed that he must; he simply could not believe that his mother would marry a man who didn't know about her son.

Calyx was aware of a certain bitterness that he held toward his mother for having told Fenbeck that he would be his apprentice in the first place. He always managed to talk himself out of it, however. *She was young,* he told himself. *She was young and desperate, and it seemed like the wise thing to do. Without Fenbeck's help over those five years when I was so young, she never would have been able to tend to everything on the farm. We would have gone without food or heat or other necessities.*

Calyx understood, but when he tried to empathize he knew that he wouldn't have done the same thing. If it were his own son, he would have found a different way to get by. But how? The traits that brought him so much success in Teversall would have been worthless in Rimmolan. Charm, good looks, and ingenuity cannot grow wheat. Each year he seemed to forget a little more about his mother. He could picture her blond hair because it was just like his, and her young, pretty face that was now eight years older. She had always been working; always figuring out how to make more money, even throughout those last few years when they had more than enough of it.

She was a farmer second and a sharp businesswoman first.

Although his scant memories of his father were hazy, he had a distinct impression that Charles was a hard worker and an honest man, while Sigrid was the driven one. He wished he could remember. He wondered if his father had worked too hard. Why did he die? A man who grew up in the country and put in a full day of physical labor every day since childhood couldn't possibly die of a fever at age twenty-three. It plagued Calyx every time he thought about it.

He didn't often think about any of it, though. Calyx hated to have pieces missing from his puzzle. He remembered the little man who made their wheat grow six feet tall, and all the money his mother made because of it, but he didn't know why the man was able to do it. Calyx had learned everything he could about plants and farming after he reached Teversall. No answers appeared in any of the books in the library. All he could recall was that he had thought the man had a magic hoe.

They reached the forest around noon this time, having left earlier than usual. He didn't know how long this visit would be, as he was completely ignorant about gem cutting. He rode Jasper into the forest and very soon Cobbkin appeared.

"How do you know when I am here?" Calyx asked, now feeling comfortable enough to inquire about things like that.

"We can sense it," Cobbkin said.

This was true, but what Cobbkin didn't elaborate on was that gnomes are capable of telepathy. Thousands of gnomes lived in the pine forest and only a few of them appeared before human tradespeople. Often, one of the other gnomes would spot Calyx coming and call to Cobbkin or to King Ghab telepathically. Since all of the animals were willingly at the service of the gnomes, it was never difficult to find a bird, a fox, or a rabbit to take Cobbkin or Ghab to Calyx quickly.

They didn't go to the Trading Tree this time. Instead, Cobbkin led Calyx to an outdoor workshop in a small clearing, bordered by an arc of trees deeper within the woods.

As he stepped in, Calyx saw a gnome-sized chair and a table holding a machine topped with two tiny wheels that were turned sideways and positioned side by side. Beside that was another table holding a device with several vertically-arranged wheels of stone in different sizes and thicknesses. Calyx gaped at the contraptions that looked nothing like the imperfectly welded, hammered-metal machinery that he was used to seeing. Not only were gnomes outstanding craftspeople, they were also brilliant innovators. Teaching a human to use those machines seemed futile to him, as nothing like that existed in Teversall. Yet he was dying to learn.

There was a larger stool, presumably for Calyx to sit on. He took a seat and Cobbkin sat at the second table, pointing to a large magnifying glass on the floor. "You will want to use that," he said. "I hope that it will be possible to teach this to you."

"Of course it will," Calyx replied with a bit of fabricated certainty.

"First," Cobbkin began, "This is a rough blue crystal. I believe you humans call it a *sapphire*." He held up a small, jagged stone that covered the entire palm of his little hand and Calyx nodded.

"It doesn't sparkle much like this. It is nice looking still, but humans like them to sparkle. The sparkle makes them valuable. Humans also like them to have extremely unnatural shapes. That also adds to the value. The first thing we must do is to shape this gem. Now, this sort of machine has not yet been invented by humans."

Calyx was amused that Cobbkin was educating him about humans, as if he weren't one of them. Cobbkin picked up another sapphire of about the same size and said, "First, we must give the bottom a subtle five-sided point at a very specific angle."

"It must be five?" Calyx asked. "Why?"

"No. It could be four or six or even three, but five is best."

Calyx accepted that as fact, although he didn't know why. Perhaps he would ask later. At the moment, he was too absorbed in watching the gem-cutting device in action to care about anything else. Cobbkin began creating the point. He secured the gem in a long and very thin pair of forceps that fastened tightly at the end. The protruding part of the stone, he pressed against the third-widest upright stone wheel and placed his foot on a pedal beneath the table. Calyx held the magnifier to the gem and as Cobbkin quickly and repeatedly pushed the pedal the wheel turned, abrading the gem.

After a moment, Cobbkin stopped and showed Calyx the straight line he had made. He turned the gem and repeated the process. "You will develop a feel for what constitutes one fifth once you have done this several times."

Calyx, to his own dismay, didn't foresee himself becoming the least bit adept at this skill, because he had no idea how to build such machines. They hadn't yet been invented, according to the gnome, and Cobbkin's foot pedal was far too small for Calyx's foot. Perhaps he could tap the wheel with his finger; however, he could not spend much time in the pine forest. It seemed odd that Cobbkin expected Calyx to make a career of gem cutting when it wouldn't be possible.

Once Cobbkin had precisely created five sides to the point, he showed it to Calyx. "It still must be buffed and polished, but this is a good base."

He flipped the gem over and displayed it from the top. "Now, Mister Overton, we wish to make them perfectly round along the side, so we go over here." He carried a pointed sapphire in each hand to the first table and poked each into one of the minuscule wheels. He tightened a clamp at the side of each and lifted an arm at the edge of the machine that moved the two wheels even closer together.

"Now, you see that the gems are touching." He sat at the chair and placed his foot on the pedal below that table. When he pumped the pedal, both of the wheels began to spin in opposite directions, forcing the sapphires to scrape against each other.

Calyx was astounded. "Did you make this machine yourself?"

"I did," Cobbkin replied with a grin. "It works very well, I must say."

After a few minutes, each stone was perfectly round when viewed from above, and the smooth rings on the sides met the pyramid base superbly.

"That was the easy part," Cobbkin told him. "Now, for the faceting."

Calyx hadn't yet noticed the black, pliable tube that pro-truded from the far end of the first machine. Cobbkin sat back in front of the many wheels and pulled the tube to his face. He took a pair of magnifying goggles off of the table and wore them at the end of his rosy, round nose. Holding the end of the tube for Ca-lyx's viewing, he said, "Do you see this flat little plane at the end of the pipe? It is coated with very rough, tiny fragments of diamond."

Calyx nodded. It looked like a piece of sandpaper covered with white sugar.

The gnome moved a third foot pedal into position. This time, he used both feet to step on it rapidly. He touched the dia-mond-coated end to the sapphire across one side until a bell rang from inside the machine. He turned the gem over and did the same to the opposite side. Then, he repeated it at ninety degrees from each of those. Methodically, he continued with touch, foot pedal, ding, turn. Touch, foot pedal, ding, turn. Dozens of times he did this until the entire gem, from the rounded sides to the center of the face, was a beautifully-symmetrical half-orb of impossibly tiny facets. It barely resembled the rough stone that Cobbkin had shown him less than an hour ago.

"Remarkable!" Calyx exclaimed.

Cobbkin was not finished. One of the larger wheels, he said, was a *buffer wheel*. It was made from a softer stone and would simply smooth any unwanted fragments and make it perfect.

Finally, he took a white wool rag, dipped it in a clear solution and carefully polished the stone, making it gleam as brightly as the emerald that Calyx had taken back to Teversall with him the previous week.

"A valuable gem," Cobbkin announced, presenting it to Calyx. "Now, because you are an excessively large creature, you will not be able to see all of the scratches and imperfections that we can see and, therefore, you cannot create a faceted gem as flawless as a gnome can create, but because your patrons are all enormous as well, it does not matter. They will not notice. A gnome, however, will always be able to tell if a gem was made by a gnome. But about the technique itself ... did you follow all of that?"

Calyx turned the jewel between his thumb and forefinger to admire its luminosity. He had watched all of it, but he wasn't sure if he had quite *followed* it. For the sake of contrast, Cobbkin placed the bumpy, duller gem beside it. "You will do this one," he said. "The base and rounding are already completed."

"How can I?" Calyx looked at the chair, into which he could not even fit his elbow.

Cobbkin frowned at him with mocking disappointment and Calyx understood. Lifting the wheeled machine and the pedals off of the small table, Calyx set them on the seat of the human-sized chair. He then sat on the ground and pressed the diamond-coated end of the black tube onto the first side of the sapphire. With his hand, Calyx pressed the pedal as quickly as he could and could not help smiling proudly when the bell gave its faint ring. With few corrections from Cobbkin, he faceted the entire top half of the jewel so that it looked almost exactly like the first one.

*This is a skill?* He thought. *Anyone could learn to do this, only because of Cobbkin's amazing machines!*

Nonetheless, Cobbkin praised him. "Congratulations. You now know how to facet gems like no other human in the world, as far as I know."

"Thank you," said Calyx. "It was a fascinating lesson. I will try to remember it, in case I ever become brilliant enough to build such machines."

Cobbkin shook his head. "It is simple physics, Mister Overton. Have you not studied physics at all?"

"Not much," he admitted. "Our schoolmaster certainly didn't teach us enough to know how to build machines like these."

"I am very surprised." Cobbkin sat in the chair by the rounding machine and leisurely threw his black-booted feet onto the table. "Mister Overton, you should never limit yourself to what the schoolmaster teaches. But then again, you do not seem like the type who does. Perhaps you have not yet been inclined to study physics. It is quite intriguing."

"It is," Calyx agreed, considering the novel suggestion that he was capable of inventing machines if he would only learn more about the sciences.

"I have more of these machines," Cobbkin continued, still leaning back in his wooden chair. "Take these with you, Mister Overton. Keep them covered up. I think you are perfectly suited as a gem cutter. It is a good trade for you."

Calyx smiled, surprised. "Sir, I couldn't take them, but I do thank you!"

"No. Take them, please. I insist. Humans have not yet invented this sort of technique. Are you a fool?"

"Whether or not I am a fool is of little consequence," Calyx replied. "I do not deserve to take your gem-cutting and gem-rounding machines with me; therefore, I cannot take them in good conscience. I would very much like to buy them from you, however, if you would agree to that."

Cobbkin pressed his lips together in thought, exposing a dimple in each of his red cheeks. "Very well, Mister Overton. You are a fool, but an honorable one. How many iolos would you like to pay for them?"

"Iolos? I thought they were worthless to you."

"Not entirely. I will take them. They can be useful to me when dealing with humans. Or I can melt them down and use the metal. What does it matter? They are of value to you, so paying me with iolos is a legitimate purchase from your perspective."

"Melting them to use the metal would be foolish," Calyx told him. "You could buy thirty times the amount of metal with them."

"Why does this bother you?" Cobbkin asked. "You are a man of business. An iolo is an iolo."

Calyx wasn't sure why it bothered him. As a man of business, he had developed the mindset necessary to trade at an advantage. Working with iolos had been straight-forward, as an iolo was the same unit to all of the people he knew. It seemed unsettling to give the gnome iolos when Cobbkin didn't even appreciate their value.

Of course he was not going to refuse, though. These machines would bring countless more iolos into his own pockets. If Cobbkin melted a pouch full of them to make a candlestick, then Cobbkin would be the foolish one. "I only have about forty with me," he said.

"Forty will suffice," Cobbkin replied, sitting up long enough to pat the table, presumably the surface on which he wanted the money to be left. "Twenty for the faceter and twenty for the rounder."

Calyx took forty iolos out of his bag and placed them before Cobbkin in a neat stack. "I don't know why you're giving me this deal, but I do appreciate it," he said.

Cobbkin smiled. He knew that Calyx would need solid gem-cutting skills in the future; it was part of the boy's course, and the little gnome felt rewarded for having played this role in it. He began to say good-bye to Calyx when the boy suddenly remembered the list his uncle had given him.

"I would like to order a few things, if that would be all right," Calyx sputtered out, relieved that he had not completely forgotten. He set the list on the table so Cobbkin could read it, each letter almost the size of Cobbkin's cap.

The gnome nodded. "Will you leave this here? We will make all of it. I already know what King Ghab would like next, so I feel safe in approving a transaction."

Calyx waited, wondering if it would be a task as bothersome as finding maps.

"Vanilla beans. We cannot get them. Also, cinnamon sticks, powder of curry and rice. We cannot grow rice. If you bring a good supply of those four things, it will be well worth your items to us."

Calyx was completely shocked. He would have very little trouble getting the items, and they would cost only a tiny fraction of the value of all of the items that Tyrone had included on his list. This trade was far too advantageous for him to accept. "Cobbkin, did you read the list? There are hundreds and hundreds of iolos worth of …"

"Mister Overton, we cannot get vanilla, cinnamon, curry, or rice. Making those things a part of the gnome society is price-less, as far as we are concerned. I implore you not to fret over it. The items that you are purchasing from us are like your rice and vanilla. You cannot get them otherwise. It is fair."

He had a point, and Calyx chose not to argue. He was leaving the forest having placed an enormous order that would be filled very easily, and with two fantastic machines that would give him a new (and, most likely, highly lucrative) proficiency. Cobbkin also handed him a pair of precision gem forceps, a bottle of the polishing fluid, and a loaf-sized burlap pouch filled with a large assortment of crystals in multiple colors and sizes.

"Learn it well," Cobbkin instructed, pointing down the road that led to Brudovel. "When you do eventually go to that place, you will see that roughly-cut gems can also be valuable to humans, but that young lady is another story."

"What young lady?"

Cobbkin smiled. "You shall find that out next year."

# Chapter 15

When Calyx showed the two gems to his uncle the following morning, he did not know what sort of reaction he should expect. As willing at Tyrone was to put just about anything on his store's shelves, Calyx knew that loose gemstones would not do. "You

did this yourself?" Tyrone asked, not quite comprehending what
had happened.

"One of them," Calyx replied. To a human, they
looked identical.

"It's astonishing," remarked Tyrone, plucking one of the
gems out of Calyx's palm. "There are so many angles. It seems
that it would take days to make it so perfect. You did this in
one afternoon?"

Calyx nodded. "I'm quite sure that each took less than an
hour. Isn't it great? I have the tools. I wish I knew what to do with
a cut gem."

"No matter, Calyx. Take some of them to the jeweler's shop
and if you would like to pursue it, Mr. Hesselink would be thrilled
to purchase them from you. He has nothing that spectacular in his
inventory and he could make some beautiful jewelry with them."

"Really?" Calyx had been apprehensive about conducting
business unrelated to Overton's Curios and was surprised that his
uncle was so nonchalant about it. Then, he wondered why he had
expected anything else. "I will do that."

"Don't tell him how you learned, though. Be mysterious
about it if you must. He knows a great deal about jewelry, so you
cannot fool him if you try to make something up. Simply state
that it is a family secret and insinuate that you learned it from

relatives on your mother's side. Nobody here knows who your mother ... was."

Calyx cringed internally. They were in the dining room and they never knew who was within earshot, but he hated pretending his mother was dead. He was weary of referring to her as his Aunt Jane and carrying on entire conversations about her with Tyrone or Clara without being able to use her real name. Even if Sigrid had made an unwise decision at one time, she didn't deserve this, nor did he.

Keeping Cobbkin's gem-cutting tools a secret was not a difficult task, as they were small enough to fit into a valise that he slid beneath his bed. The housemaids would never look inside it when they cleaned, and rarely did anyone disturb him when he was in his bedroom. He was concerned, however, about the noise that the machines would make.

He went into the basement to look for a grindstone or some other noisy machine that he could take to his room as a sound decoy. Once there, he decided that the basement was the best place to work. The servants only went into the basement a couple times a day and Tyrone would tell them to stay upstairs when Calyx was working. They would not think much about that and the noise would never travel to their ears.

He cordoned off a section of the basement and walked the two floors to get the valise, the rough gems, the polishing fluid, and the iron tongs from his room.

Positioning the tiny foot pedals on the table, he set to work, two jewels at a time. First, he created the pointed bases, rounding out the sides into neat circles and then working dozens of facets onto the face, just as Cobbkin taught him. It was odd that Calyx remembered every step as if he had watched gnomes do this for years ... as if he himself had cut gems for years. He didn't have to think. Calyx was always a quick learner, but never before had he learned something without having to think.

He completed six that afternoon and he had to get back to the shop, so he packed all of his utensils into the valise and took it back to his room. The six finished and polished gems he dropped into a tiny velvet pouch that he found in his uncle's office. He took them with him, rehearsing mentally his approach when he would speak with Mr. Hesselink.

The jeweler was intrigued and delighted. The man had been working with jewelry for over thirty years and the cut of the gems bewildered him. He held them up and watched the sun's radiance bounce off of them in every direction. He inspected them carefully with a jeweler's loupe. He scraped the pointed ends of each gem onto a sheet of glass, already quite scratched up. He determined that they were genuine.

Out of sheer pride in his own perceived expertise, Mr. Hesselink did not ask how the young, inexperienced gem cutter did it. "Mr. Overton, these are very handsome stones. Quite flawless and I have never seen anything so brilliant. You have found a new customer. How much do you ask for all six?"

Calyx had researched the price of gems relative to size, but as Cobbkin had pointed out, the faceting was what made them more valuable. He threw out a number. "I would like seventy each, Mr. Hesselink."

The jeweler's eyes widened at the price, but Calyx did not waver. "The diamond is the same price as the topaz?" he asked, perplexed.

"Yes," said Calyx, not wishing to price each gem individually. The gnomes didn't seem to make a distinction, but perhaps they just didn't know any better. "At this time, they are all the same," he clarified, to allow for any future policy changes.

Assuming that the boy had procured them from a distant land and that he had spent days meticulously cutting each of them, Mr. Hesselink agreed. Almost. "Will you take four hundred for the six?"

"I will," Calyx readily nodded.

Calyx walked out of the jeweler's shop feeling as rich as a king. He had been living well in the Overton home, but this was the first time he had ever earned a large sum of money completely independent of the curio shop. He felt liberated and worthy.

Just to gauge the amount of interest the new jewelry would generate among his customers, Mr. Hesselink proceeded to make a simple gold ring with each of the small gems. As he had hoped and anticipated, the customers were astounded, and some of the wealthiest felt that they had to have something made with those marvelously faceted stones. They didn't want to buy the rings, however. They wanted to place orders for custom-made pieces. He told them that he would see what he could do.

Very soon, Calyx had a great deal of work to do. Within a week, Mr. Hesselink requested diamonds, rubies, and emeralds in a variety of sizes, and customers continued to inquire. Hesselink Jewelers soon became just as fashionable in Teversall as Overton's Curios ever had been.

Calyx had always planned to send money to his mother when he was able to earn it on his own. Even if she would not move to Teversall, she could vacate her position at the duke's manor and live comfortably in a country cottage somewhere. Calyx had wanted to do this for her for years, but now she needed nothing. It was undoubtedly a fortunate problem to have, but it still seemed sadly ironic that *now* he had money to give to her.

With Calyx serving as second-to-chief at Overton's Curios and an enterprising gem cutter, Tyrone gave him his own office area at the back of the shop. It was only a mahogany desk, two chairs, and a filing case but it made things much easier for Calyx, now that he had clients to meet with on an almost daily basis.

He could see the register counter from his desk, so his sociable nature was not stifled when someone interesting came into the shop. Often, he would rise to greet a customer or answer questions about inventory that would be available in the near future. His natural charisma made him a favorite among the townspeople of Teversall, and some of them would come in just to chat with Calyx.

In the early mornings and evenings, he worked on the jeweler's custom orders. He finished most of that work after four days. On the fifth, Tyrone gave him a stack of balance sheets to work on at his desk in the shop. He started to go over them while his uncle stood at the register.

"Thaumatropes," Calyx mumbled, wondering if they needed to order more of those popular toys from London. The kids seemed fascinated with the illusion that the pictures made, and he projected that they would continue to sell them steadily throughout the summer. None of the sheets listed the inventory for that item, so he got up and walked to the storage room.

*Only eight more. We'd better order another twenty or so,* he concluded.

As he closed the door and began to walk back to his desk, he faintly heard an odd tenor of a voice from the front of the store. It was a voice he knew, but he couldn't quite place who it was. He glanced toward the desk and saw a very undersized man talking to Tyrone. The face barely cleared the edge of the counter and it was quite a distance from the storage room entrance, but he recognized the creaking voice; the bulging, amber-colored eyes; and the thin, snickering lips.

He stayed out of view and crept along the side of the room to get a better look from behind a shelf.

It was Fenbeck.

# Chapter 16

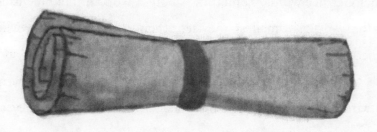

Fenbeck was only engaging Tyrone in general conversation, but his eyes darted all over the store as he talked. Calyx wondered if his mother had ever described him to Tyrone. What did they know about him? They had never discussed it at length with Calyx and now he wished they had. His uncle didn't seem at all uneasy about chatting with the little man.

Calyx struggled to decide how to handle it. Should he burst onto the scene and confront Fenbeck? Should he wait and find out what he was up to? Then a thought hit him. Had Sigrid been warning him about this in her strange letter? He tried to remember her words. Something about a woman in a blue dress. Buttons were too small, so they sent them to Teversall. He wished he had the letter to refer to, right then.

The last time Fenbeck saw Calyx, the boy was eight years old with blonde hair to his shoulders. Now, he was a sixteen-year-old young man. His hair was quite a bit darker and much shorter. He didn't think he could be easily recognized, even by a semi-magical creature.

Calyx left a quick note for his uncle. *Will return shortly.* He stepped through the back door of the shop and walked around the building, watching the front entrance from just beyond the corner. A moment later, Fenbeck walked out and headed across the street, clutching a diminutive golden-handled cane in his left hand, with a velvet sack slung over his shoulder. Once there was some distance between them, Calyx followed him.

He had to stay out of earshot, in case Fenbeck knew his new name. Everyone in Teversall knew Calyx and someone would certainly call out to greet him in this public setting. He kept all of his focus on tracking the elf, who walked through the park and sat at a bench beside a peasant woman in a ratty grey shawl.

They were talking. Calyx suddenly decided to take a risk and get closer. He crept behind the trees at the back of the bench and, when nobody was facing his direction, he scooted into the brush and quietly stepped behind them, completely engulfed in the foliage of a gigantic wisteria vine. He could see a little, and he could hear.

Fenbeck pulled a roll of parchment out of his velvet sack and showed it to the woman. It was a document. Calyx couldn't see the small print, but he saw the words *Charles Blythe, Jr.* and a signature at the bottom: *Sigrid Blythe.*

His mother had never signed anything. He knew that. Fenbeck read the paper to the peasant woman, but Calyx could barely understand him. The woman shrugged her shoulders. Then Fenbeck said, "The lad, I believe, might be a relative of the Overton family. He owes me a year of servitude, and a good citizen would help me find him. Would you know of a young lad in that family?"

Again, the woman shrugged her shoulders, not saying a word the entire time. Finally, the elf stood, snorted ungratefully at her and made his way across the park. Calyx waited until it was safe to emerge from the bushes, and when he did, the peasant woman turned her face and looked directly at him.

It was Mrs. Wrigley.

"Stay," she said.

"Stay? No. I have to follow him."

Sternly, she pushed her hand out and glanced across the park. "Are you the one he is looking for, Mr. Overton?"

Now Calyx was trapped. How could he deny it? "I am not sure," he said. "Was my name on the paper?"

She shook her head, knowingly. "No. It was not. He must be mistaken. Have your uncle draw up your birth certificate immediately. Do that now. Do not follow the Borgh elf."

Although Calyx didn't know what a Borgh elf was, he nodded. He didn't have time to ask questions and he knew that Mrs. Wrigley was no fool. He left the park and dashed back to Overton's Curios, where his uncle was still at the counter, talking to an employee. "Uncle," he said, "please, I must speak with you in private."

Tyrone followed him to his own secure office and closed the door. "What is it, Calyx? You look upset."

Calyx took a deep breath. Even at a distressing time like this, he didn't want to look upset. "Uncle, the small man who came in earlier … that was the horrible little man who worked for my mother in Rimmolan. He is looking for me. He has a document with my mother's name forged onto it. Do I have a birth certificate?"

He recoiled at hearing his own voice say it. Calyx rarely lied. In fact, he had never told an untruth to his uncle or aunt, but he had been lying to everyone else about his own identity for eight years. He had been lying so consistently that he had begun to believe the lies himself. Now he was asking for a false birth certificate … a forged document to confirm his lies.

Yet this dishonesty was all he had to defeat the evil that pursued him. It was justified.

Gravely yet urgently, Tyrone nodded. "You do. You are my late brother's son and they turned the papers over to me when my brother died. We have it at the house. I will go right now and get it, to keep it safe. You stay back here."

"I'm not afraid of him. If I have a birth certificate, he can't have me arrested. He says that I owe him a year of servitude. Perhaps he won't even figure out who I am."

Tyrone wasted no time leaving the store. Calyx stood behind the register, helping customers as if nothing out of the ordinary had passed.

For years, he had awakened during the night with dreams about that awful, impish creature, but only in his dreams. While

Calyx was awake, he had no fear of him. Tyrone had no crops to destroy. Fenbeck was barely four feet tall. There was nothing to fear, as long as the law was on Calyx's side. At least this is what he kept telling himself.

When Tyrone reached the house, he began to dig through the documents in his safe. Clara heard him and entered the room. "Tyrone, it's in there," she said, lowering her voice to a whisper. "I'm on guard. Mrs. Winston came by today and said that a strange man was looking for Charlie Blythe."

He stared at her, aghast.

"Of course, I didn't react at all to the name. I have never heard of that person."

"Nor have I," he asserted, taking the birth certificate out of the safe.

Tyrone contemplated whether or not the document would be safer in his pocket than in the iron safe, which was nearly two inches thick at each wall and weighed hundreds of pounds. He placed the paper back inside it, locked the door of the safe, and dropped the key into his pocket. They had nothing to worry about. Nobody would believe the elf.

He went back to the shop and kept an eye on Calyx for the rest of the day, checking his pocket continuously for the key.

When they returned to the house that evening, Calyx went straight to his room to reexamine the letter from his mother.

*Martha visited last week in her new azure silk gown. She said that the undersized buttons were here in Stratskon, but did not suit my wardrobe, so they are en route to Teversall to Clara Overton. Please let them know so that you all might be expecting the arrival.*

There was no Martha. Did she just make that up for content? Undersized buttons could symbolize Fenbeck. Of course. Fenbeck had been in Stratskon, presumably tracking down Sigrid. When he didn't find Calyx there, he headed for Teversall. Calyx was supposed to warn Tyrone and Clara.

*How could I have been so stupid?* He hadn't said a word to his aunt and uncle because he didn't think it would make any more sense to them. But then again, they just would have worried. What could anyone have done about it?

Tyrone closed all of the parlor curtains that evening. Calyx took the letter to him and apologized. "I should have shown it to you rather than simply relay the message about Aunt Jane's marriage," he said.

"It's all right, dear boy," Tyrone replied, gravely sliding his gilt-rimmed spectacles down to the tip of his nose and reading the letter by the light of a crystal lamp. He read it a few times and then nodded with eyes upturned toward Calyx. "It seems to make sense now. Doesn't it? I wouldn't have made anything of it either. Don't feel badly."

The two walked to the curio shop as they always did the next morning. Mrs. Wrigley came in as soon as they opened the front door. She had a cruet set to sell, but it seemed to Calyx that it was only an excuse to visit the shop. There were no customers there yet. She placed the set on the counter and said, "Ten iolos?"

Tyrone began to inspect the items and her eyes met Calyx's. She handed him a small, folded piece of paper, which he read at his desk while Tyrone bartered with her.

Borgh elf. In forest near Lyman farm. Must find his true name.

The only part of this that Calyx understood was the part about the Lymans' farm. He knew where that was. He already knew Fenbeck's name, and if the fact that it was a Borgh elf meant anything, the significance escaped him. She had also used the term the other day. He wondered if he should ask, but decided against it, not wanting to endanger the kind old woman any further than she was already endangering herself.

He folded the slip of paper back up and shoved it into his trouser pocket, rejoining them at the register. Tyrone was paying her, and the look on his face told Calyx that she had said something to him.

When Mrs. Wrigley left, Tyrone turned to Calyx. "She just saw him waiting at the steps of the council with that document in his hand."

A customer walked in and the two went about their business, but when Tyrone stepped into the back of the shop, Calyx showed him the paper. He didn't want to keep things from his uncle anymore.

# Chapter 17

Sigrid could barely swallow her tea as she sat daintily in the drawing room with her soon-to-be lady-in-waiting, Louisa. Thea had come back earlier in the day, again dressed in blue, but this time disguised as a seamstress.

Thea had dropped off a stack of crisp linen napkins, asking to see the lady of the house. When Sigrid met with her and sorted through the linens, Thea said, "I am taking some of these to Teversall in the morning." She lowered her chirpy voice to an almost silent whisper. "I know you must be anxious. I have a plan." She winked and left the manor with a few napkins still in her hands.

"Lady Jane, would you like any pastries?" Louisa asked, noting the distracted expression on Sigrid's face.

"Oh, no, thank you," she replied, sipping her tea. "I feel a little tired. I think I will lie down for a while."

She excused herself from the drawing room and went to her chamber to think. What could that strange person's plan be? The lady from the forest, whose name she didn't even know ... it was so perplexing, but she felt that the mysterious lady in blue truly would help if she could. She had to believe it.

Sir Geoffrey would be home soon. He knew nothing about her son. She never went more than an hour without feeling that pang of guilt for not telling him, but she had always wanted, above all, to protect her little Charlie. Now he was grown to nearly a man and she wasn't even sure what he looked like anymore. She would have given anything to see him.

She was angry. She had denied him a mother, both of them had taken on false lives and disrespected the memory of Charles Senior just to avoid this horrid little Borgh elf creature, and now it seemed that it was all for naught. He found them anyway. He would try to get what he considered his due however he could. She was angry at him and, most of all, angry at herself for having even been so foolish.

*I should be a pauper,* she thought. *I don't deserve to be enjoying all this luxury.* She wanted to leave, to go to Teversall and reclaim her son, but he didn't need a mother anymore. She scowled fiercely at the window that looked out upon the road that led to Rimmolan, or to Borgh. Her only comfort was in knowing that the Overtons had been good to Calyx.

And he had some sort of fairy power. She remembered Thea mentioning that. He was a bright, strong, capable young man apparently capable of dryadic magic. As angry as she was, she focused on him. Calyx would understand her letter. He would know what to do.

Thea quickly took the form of a kingfisher and flew toward Teversall. She knew that it wouldn't be easy to convince the disinterested dryads of that land to help a human, but she must at least try or she would never forgive herself. The other fairies of Rimmolan would never forgive her either.

As she sailed over the rolling meadows and wooded hills, she tried to remember everything she had ever heard about the Borgh elves. They were rarely seen in Rimmolan and, therefore, seldom discussed. Still, every few years, someone would mention one of them, and it was never pleasant. They were cunning, incredibly strong, and wonderfully talented. They could have contributed a great deal to society and found themselves highly respected if they weren't so teeming with bitterness.

Suddenly, Thea thought of something that had not occurred to her before. Every spell a fairy ever casts must be reversible. It is part of the law of magic: Nothing can go in one direction with no possibility of ever returning.

Thea recalled one particular bit of information she had once heard about the Borgh elves. When the fairies of Borgh initially cast the spell on the beavers, they gave each of them a never-before-used name that was to be kept secret. The elves then chose false names for themselves. She wasn't sure whether they were aware of their true names or not, but it was said that if a human guessed that name in the elf's presence, the spell would be broken. The elf would revert to a life as a common beaver.

Thea was amazed that she had never thought of it before. If this was true, then it was worth looking into. But how would she learn Fenbeck's name? Perhaps nobody knew it. Fenbeck certainly wouldn't tell it to anyone.

Quickly, she took a sharp turn to the left and headed toward Borgh. The fairies there might not be able to divulge that information. They may have forgotten it.

It was a long shot, but she had to try.

**Later that day,** Calyx and Tyrone walked home from Overton's Curios. They still felt a bit anxious, but since they had not seen Fenbeck at all that day, the unease had subsided just a little. They entered through the main corridor, systematically hung their hats, and removed their coats. Clara met them in the parlor with inquisitive blue eyes.

Tyrone nodded to his wife with a half smile. "All is well today."

As he had done that morning and the previous day, Tyrone pulled the key out of his pocket and went to check the safe. Calyx headed toward the kitchen to see the cooks, as he was famished. They had a quiet dinner, discussing little other than how good the roast mutton was.

Just before dawn the next morning, Calyx was still upstairs, almost ready to head down to the dining room for breakfast. He had just closed his door and reached the top of the staircase when he heard his uncle's voice roar.

"The safe!"

Calyx's feet barely touched the floor as he ran down to the office. All of the servants rushed there as well, and they all gasped to see that the window was wide open.

The safe was gone.

Tyrone stuck his head and shoulders through the window, looking to the left and right. It didn't seem humanly possible for anyone to get that enormously heavy safe through the window. "Guard Calyx," Tyrone quickly ordered everyone else. "I am going for help." He rushed out of the office.

Calyx dashed through the door behind him, ignoring the calls from the others. He ran through the front entrance of the house without grabbing his hat or coat and Tyrone was already halfway down the road.

Calyx went into the stable and led Jasper out of it, hurrying the horse away before anyone could try to stop them. He rode out of the village, thankful for the nearly full moon still hovering in the grey darkness, and traveled three miles down the gravel road toward the property of the Lyman family.

He stopped Jasper near their cow pasture and tied him to a tree, silently continuing along the edge of the woods. He was no spy. Perhaps Fenbeck saw him coming. He didn't care. His mother had been afraid of the corrupt, nasty imp, but he wasn't. He intended to take care of the problem directly.

*In the forest,* Mrs. Wrigley's note had indicated. Not along the edge of it, but *in* it. Calyx stepped between a pair of birch trees and entered, squinting his eyes briefly in an attempt to adjust them for the impending darkness of the wilderness, as the sun still had not completely come up. Borgh elves probably had excellent night vision. Fenbeck seemed like a nocturnal sort.

No matter. Calyx's eyes adjusted. He crept lightly, making very little noise, and slowly scanned the woods around him for signs of the elf. A skunk scampered in front of Calyx's feet, almost tripping him. A coyote howled, not too far in the distance. He continued on, patiently and steadily. He had all day.

He reached an area from which he could see a very small clearing. It looked like someone had been there quite recently. He saw a pile of sticks stacked up beside something that looked like a fire pit. It was difficult to tell in the dark. It couldn't have been there for long. The sticks seemed to be stacked too neatly.

He heard a low growl just a few yards away from him. It stopped. Then another. He turned in its direction, but saw nothing. It didn't sound like a bear or a wildcat. It was coming from the ground. He crept closer, his heart almost pounding out of his ribcage.

At once, he learned the answer to a question he had recently pondered. Borgh elves were not nocturnal, nor were they exceptionally early risers. Fenbeck lay on a bed of dexterously-woven sticks, sound asleep, and it was nearly six a.m.

Calyx stared down at him in disbelief. Was the elf faking? He watched him for several minutes and concluded that nobody could act that convincingly. It was odd for Calyx, who had been, more or less, dominated for years by his family's fear of this horrid scoundrel, to suddenly find himself in the position to kill him.

He could, easily. He was nearly twice his size and Fenbeck was absolutely scrawny. But Calyx, despite his anger, could not even consider doing it.

For several weeks, he had been analyzing the hints from Mrs. Wrigley. She seemed to be suggesting that Calyx had some unique quality about him, but he had no idea what it was. She insinuated it when she told him to trade with the gnomes directly. King Ghab and Cobbkin seemed to confirm it when they decided that he was *the one* who could be taught to facet jewels. He even felt it sometimes, though he had virtually forgotten about the big blue bee. Whenever things became difficult, he felt a force inside him suddenly emerge, as if it had a voice of its own.

Here it was.

"Borgh elf," he whispered, too softly to wake Fenbeck, but loudly enough, he hoped, for him to hear it subconsciously. "Borgh elf, what is your true name?"

The snoring continued.

Calyx moved closer. "Borgh elf, what is your true name?"

Fenbeck continued to snore, but his narrow, languid mouth pinched together, as if a spider had crawled across his face. Perhaps it had.

Calyx asked him several times. He didn't answer. Finally, Fenbeck stirred and rolled partly over, mumbling incoherently. Frustrated that he might have just misunderstood the answer, Calyx asked again, in a rather irritated tone.

That time, the beady, orangey eyes quickly opened, staring directly at the boy. The gaunt face suddenly filled with rage and the Borgh elf's lip formed a slow, delighted smile.

"Hello, Charlie."

# Chapter 18

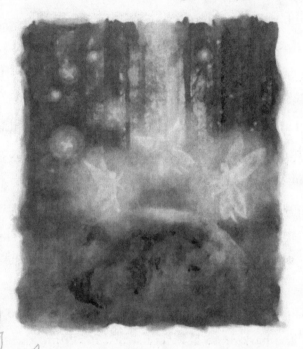

The land of Borgh felt eerie and desolate to Thea as she soared above the river. There were beavers along the bank, with lodges here and there, but not as many as she had expected. There were a few families of elves living in snug wooden cottages within a mile of the river, presumably as farmers. Their fields were lush and magnificent, but it seemed that the elves would have no way to earn money from it. Borgh was extremely remote. Thea wondered who ate all that food.

The willows, young oaks, and rowan trees stood in various stages of regrowth. They sent up new shoots after having been felled by the beavers. Beyond the bank of the river, the forest became increasingly thick and tall. Thea dipped down into the woodland and flew between the trees, deep into the wilderness.

She had seen the elves in their fields and she knew that the dryads must have retreated rather far into the forest to stay away from them, but she did not know how far. The forest trees, like dark and commanding prisms, allowed the sun to hit the ground in silvery streaks of light, but it wasn't peaceful like the forest of Rimmolan. She could never feel at ease here.

About four miles into the woods, she began to see signs of them. The bark of an alder construed itself into the shape of a running horse's face, its mane hovering in the air. Beside that tree, a beech presented an image of a bream minnow jumping out of a lake. A human might not even notice. More likely, a human would call it a coincidence. Only a dryad like Thea would know what these images meant.

She landed with both feet on a prominent bough in the middle of the alder and cocked her head, her beak pointing up the center of the tree. She wanted to have a look at the dryads of Borgh before they saw her. She hopped to a higher branch, then to a higher one. Finally, nearly at the top of the tree, she could see the dryad of the alder, leaning back on a leafy pillow.

They didn't look much like the fairies of Rimmolan, or other fairies that she had known. These were dull in color, blending with the trees, yet they carried a decidedly lucid glow of life. They seemed completely serious about being dryads.

Thea took a deep breath. *If I could talk to a human twice, I can certainly do this,* she told herself. She disposed of the bird disguise and tried to control her blue glow as she cautiously flew upward toward the resting dryad.

Thea cleared her throat politely. The dryad in the alder opened her eyes and Thea was relieved to see that she wasn't frightened. "Greetings," said the dryad.

"Hello. I am Thea, from the forest of Rimmolan."

"I am Kiri," the dryad replied. "Why have you come so far?"

Three more fairies arrived and encircled Thea, smiling peacefully. She had obviously disrupted all of their daily routines, but they didn't seem to mind. From Thea's observation, their routines didn't consist of much. As she began to talk, more and more of them appeared. She continued her speech, addressing them all.

"I came because of an urgent matter. There is a young man who was born in Rimmolan and now lives in Teversall. He has a minuscule amount of dryad blood, but it is enough to make him worth a great deal to some. There is a Borgh elf who knows about him and wants to use the lad's dryad power to transform him into an elf. He is my responsibility. I need your help."

"What can we do?" a pallid birch fairy asked with a sigh. They had, over the years, heard of two other enchanted humans who had been brought back to this land and turned into Borgh elves. "We have relinquished power over them. If they come here, we cannot do anything."

"They are both in Teversall," Thea replied. "Am I correct in believing that the Borgh elf will revert to the form of a beaver if his name is spoken aloud in his presence?"

Another fairy nodded, catching Thea's attention. "It is true. Does the boy know the elf's name?"

Thea pressed her lips together. These dryads were not as intelligent as those she was accustomed to. "No. Will you give me his name?"

"We would, but we don't know which one he is."

"He calls himself Fenbeck," Thea said, hoping that would jog their memory. All of them stared back at Thea with blank faces. Clearly, they wanted to go back to their tree homes and take naps. Trying to hide her frustration, Thea forced a sweet smile. "Is there any way that you can help me determine this particular elf's name?"

In unison, they all shook their heads. "There are hundreds of elf names," Kiri explained, sympathetically. We have a list of names, but no descriptions of any of the elves. Nobody recorded the names that they gave themselves. I am sorry that we can't tell you what his true name is. The only way we could do that would be to go there ourselves and ask the tree witnesses."

*Ask the trees?* Thea had never heard it worded quite that way, but it gave her a glimmer of hope. Before she could make the suggestion, many of the dryads began to nod at each other and chit-chat in murmurs. Thea looked at Kiri, curiously.

"And we shall," Kiri told her, hopping off her branch and fluttering in the air indomitably. "Thea, lead us to Teversall!"

# Chapter 19

Calyx froze for a few seconds as those beady eyes glared at him. Fenbeck didn't seem the least bit startled for having been asleep just seconds ago. Calyx would not allow himself to be intimidated. "You will leave Teversall and stay away from us forever," he said, as if he were telling him a fact.

Fenbeck laughed. His eyes darted at the ground and a vine shot out of the soil beneath Calyx, wrapping itself around his ankle. Calyx lurched forward, but in an instant, the plant held both feet firmly in place. He pulled his leg up with all his might. In response, the vine thickened.

Satisfied that the boy would be going nowhere for a few minutes, Fenbeck held up his knobby index finger. "I shall bring the carriage around, Charlie. We are going to Borgh. It'll be quick and painless. Trust me. Afterward, you will be as content as I am."

Calyx glared at Fenbeck fiercely, but said nothing. He saw no reason to detain him for conversation about the matter. He had a knife in his pocket, and his hands were free. Fenbeck snickered in self-satisfaction and hurried off to get the carriage.

Quickly, Calyx grabbed the knife and began to cut away at the vine. It continued to grow and entangle him. His efforts seemed useless. A tiny fleck of red then appeared from behind the kindling pile. Calyx strained his eyes with hope.

It was the hat of a gnome.

King Ghab scuttled around the sticks and hopped right onto one of the vine's tendrils. It began to loosen. "Mister Overton, you must listen to me," he said, waving off any expression of surprise that he found on Calyx's face. There was no time to explain.

Calyx smiled. "Thank you, King."

"He's coming," Ghab suddenly whispered. "Pretend to still be trapped until he turns his back. I will keep the plants and animals from ensnaring you. They cannot obey a Borgh elf when I am present. Now listen, Mister Overton. Use the power that you received when the bee stung you … the power the blue dryad gave you. Indeed, the dryads are coming. You must communicate with them through nature."

Calyx's eyes widened in bewilderment. He wasn't even sure what a dryad was, but he knew it wasn't a bee, and he remembered having been stung by a blue bee a long time ago. Was King Ghab saying that the bee had given him some sort of power? "How do I communicate with them?" he asked.

Ghab shook his head. The hooves of Fenbeck's horses hit the ground not far away. There was no time. "Do it," Ghab said, and he ran back behind the pile of sticks.

Calyx could have run, but that wouldn't have solved the problem. Fenbeck would continue to lurk and taunt Calyx and his family. He had to stay and see to it that the nightmare would come to an end. Having Ghab there to advise him made that seem entirely possible.

Fenbeck led the carriage through the woods, weaving it through spaces large enough to fit. As he drew nearer, he pushed an oak tree completely out of his way, just to intimidate Calyx, in case he was thinking about trying to fight with him. The tree fell, its roots protruding from the ground like a snarled medley of petrified snakes. Fenbeck kicked them with the heel of his polished black boot.

He walked toward Calyx with a thick straw rope over his shoulder and reached his hands toward the boy's foot, grabbing onto the root of the vine. "Guess who braided this straw when he was a little boy," he sneered, showing Calyx the golden rope. "Guess who grew the wheat. It's the best, strongest wheat that could possibly be grown. Your mother did a fine job with the plaiting, Charlie. A fine job."

Calyx was careful to keep his feet within the vine, as if it were still holding him. Fenbeck pulled the thick roots out of the ground and unrolled half the rope, preparing to tie Calyx up and drag him to the carriage.

The sun was up, but the sky above them abruptly darkened enough to prompt both of them to look upward. Hundreds of tiny, fluttering fairies hovered above the trees, their earthen-toned bodies edged with copper coronas against the sun. They began to descend and disappear into the forest like drops of rain. Fenbeck shrieked and his hands shook as he rushed toward Calyx with the rope. Calyx leaped, freeing his feet and ankles from the vine spiral.

He knew that these fairies were the dryads that Ghab had referred to. He had to communicate with them through nature. Somehow.

Thea, the only blue object in the forest, fluttered resolutely to the tree that was knocked onto its side and ordered it to stand up. It stood and the ground sealed itself back up around its roots as if it had never fallen.

Fenbeck shrieked again, to see his own deed so easily undone by a fairy. He was fast and he was strong, but he was far too flustered to catch Calyx. Fenbeck fixed his eyes on the ferns, the trees, the ground, trying to create another entanglement to hold the boy in place, but nothing cooperated.

Calyx watched Thea intently, aware that she was the one who would help him communicate. To his knowledge he had never seen a fairy before, but he was quite certain that he had met with this creature. Blue. She floated in front of the same tree, holding Calyx's attention, and he focused all of his thought onto what she might be trying to say.

The bark of the tree began to move, its lines contorting into curves and finally, into letters. A word. Calyx glanced around the forest.

In a moment, every tree within his view was marked with the same word.

Fenbeck gripped the sides of his head with both hands, sobbing in agony. He looked from left to right as if trying to escape the message that surrounded him. "No! Mr. Blythe, do not. Do not!"

"Orgollath," Calyx read.

With one long, horrified shriek, the Borgh elf clenched his bony fists as he shrank to the earth floor and became what he had been at birth: an unassuming, honest brown beaver.

It looked at Calyx ambivalently, beat its tail on the ground a few times, clicked its teeth together and scurried off into the forest to look for a river. Just like that.

Without allowing themselves to be thanked or praised, the dryads lifted off to return to their tree homes in Borgh. Thea hid at the top of an oak tree and listened for a while, leaving Calyx to believe that she had flown away with the others.

Ghab smiled proudly. "Mister Overton, I knew that you could do it. Good job!"

Calyx still wasn't entirely sure what had just happened. "He is ... a beaver?"

"Yes, yes. A Borgh elf. He's far from Borgh, though. He will have to find a beaver colony here to take him in. He's quite harmless now, Mister Overton. Well done!"

"What did I do?" Calyx scratched his head, half laughing.

"You focused. You used your power. You are part dryad, you know."

"I am not!"

"You are. We all know it. Cobbkin could tell right away. You just proved it by interpreting the elf's true name. What are the odds of guessing a name like that?"

"I didn't guess," Calyx contradicted him incredulously. "It's written all over the trees!"

Ghab nodded, joyfully. "It's not, my boy. I can't see it. I have no dryad power. To me, it looked like a guess. I thought that one of the dryads had whispered it to you. How wonderful!"

Calyx moved his eyes across the woods, still seeing the word *Orgollath* in the bark of every tree. He wondered if it would still look like that if he returned in a week.

"Thank you very, very much, King Ghab. If you ever need anything, remember that I owe you. I wish I could thank the dryads."

"They know," Ghab said.

"Now," Calyx took a deep breath. "I must decide how to tell my aunt and uncle! What should I say? The truth seems so far-fetched."

"Isn't that always the way with humans?" Ghab laughed. "You'll think of something."

Calyx bid his wise little friend good-bye and left the forest. Jasper was still waiting patiently by the field. In satisfied silence, the young man untied him and rode home.

# Chapter 20

When Calyx arrived back at the manor, both his aunt and his uncle were at the council building, where Fenbeck had filed an official proclamation that Calyx should be turned over to him. They reported the safe missing, of course, and called for Fenbeck to be arrested and investigated for theft.

Teversall did not have an organized police department, but the members of the community looked out for one another. Friends and neighbors who had risen early were scouring the town for signs of Calyx and the elf. Tyrone and Clara met with a detective who knew nothing about Borgh elves or tree fairies.

Arthur the footman smiled happily when he saw Calyx on the familiar silver Barb. He greeted the boy quickly and ran off to inform Clara and Tyrone that their boy had returned.

The three of them sat in the parlor an hour later. With a new energy that overtook his physical and mental exhaustion, Calyx took their hands in his and smiled. "Aunt and Uncle, I can tell you with certainty that our troubles are over. He will not be back."

They both beamed. "What happened?" Clara asked.

"I cannot tell you," Calyx replied. The last thing he wanted was to burden them with too much information. The whole town would soon know about the morning's confusion and people would be asking them. Calyx considered it kinder to let them remain sincerely ignorant of the facts so that they wouldn't have to lie anymore. "I can only tell you that he is gone. It is all over. You must take my word for it"

Clara grabbed Tyrone's arm joyfully, and then she pulled Calyx into an embrace. "That is wonderful! Calyx, you're free! Your Aunt Jane ... *Sigrid* ... is free!"

That had just begun to dawn on Calyx. He could barely remember what it had felt like as a young boy to be free from the threat of Fenbeck. Everything should seem different, but somehow, he felt almost the same.

"We have to tell your mother," Tyrone said. "Perhaps she will know soon. It seems that she has some sort of informant. Still, let's plan a trip to Stratskon soon, if she approves.

*If she approves.* Calyx wasn't sure how to respond to that.

Nevertheless, it was a festive occasion in the Overton home. Tyrone did not open the shop all day. He gave all of his employees a paid day off and he didn't care how much money he lost. They had letters to write and much to discuss; he didn't want to be bothered with business matters on the best day of his life. That afternoon, Calyx sat on a rocking chair on the side porch and allowed himself to take it all in.

He had spent the latter half of his life feeling bitter. If the elf had never come along, Calyx's life wouldn't have been disrupted. His mother wouldn't have had to work as a housekeeper. She would have been able to raise him. That constant resentment had followed Calyx everywhere he had gone, even though he had generally been happy living in Teversall.

Now, he realized that the elf had only pursued him because the dryads had somehow given him some of their power. He could almost as easily have reasoned that if the *fairies* had never come along, his life wouldn't have been disrupted.

Perhaps they were to blame.

He leaned back in the chair and looked at the familiar well-kept houses across the street. *This is my life,* he thought. *My course. Perhaps it hasn't been disrupted at all.*

Although he felt guilty, knowing that it had caused his mother so much pain, Calyx was also, in some ways, glad that the whole ordeal had occurred. Had the fairies and the Borgh elf never come along, he wouldn't have become as educated as he was. He would have been obligated to work as a farmer on a remote plot of land in an even more remote town. He wouldn't have learned anything about trade. He wouldn't know how to facet gems like a gnome. He would never have met the gnomes at all. This was his life, and he felt comfortable in it.

He liked to believe that even his mother was better off. She was rich now, and if she loved her new husband, she would not be lonely. He would never recover entirely from having lost all those years with her, but perhaps it was her course.

The entrance to the house opened and out walked Tyrone. He sat in the other rocking chair and allowed Calyx to continue with his thoughts for a few minutes. Then, he said, "If you would like to go to Stratskon to live, we completely understand."

Calyx turned his tired face toward him. "Stratskon? Oh, no. I haven't even thought of that. May I stay here, Uncle?"

"Of course!" Tyrone's eyes welled up with tears of relief. "You would be sorely missed by your aunt and myself … and everyone else. Calyx, you are welcome to stay as long as you wish to. Your aunt and I are both incredibly proud of what you have become. Incredibly proud!"

"Thank you."

Calyx couldn't imagine leaving Teversall. He loved his mother, but he didn't know her as a mother anymore. Clara was his mother. Tyrone was his father. Teversall was his home. He would like to visit Stratskon, if Sigrid would allow it. He had doubts that Sir Geoffrey even knew that he had a stepson.

"Another thing," Tyrone began. "If you would like to go by your birth name, I will send to Rimmolan for your birth record. It is up to you, and we respect any decision you make."

Calyx tried to imagine himself as Charlie Blythe. He should honor his father and carry on the family name, but it was another thing from his past, so far back into his childhood that he couldn't reach it. It was something that he no longer was, like a moth trying to turn back into a caterpillar. "I feel that my name is Calyx Overton, if that is all right with you," he said, "but it would be wonderful to have the birth record anyway."

Tyrone nodded. He, like Calyx, was a man who did not like loose ends. He intended to tie all of it up as neatly as possible.

The two sat for an hour, not conversing much at all, but addressing various questions as they came up. Calyx wanted to go back to Rimmolan and see what had become of their farm house. It still legally belonged to Sigrid, as far as he knew. He wanted to see some of the belongings of his childhood. He remembered the books. He wanted to walk into the workroom where he and his mother plaited straw. He wanted to see the walls that his father had built. He hoped that someone had maintained the skillfully thatched roof.

# Chapter 21

So he remained Calyx Overton, of Teversall. He continued to work in his uncle's shop, to cut gems for the jeweler, and to trade with the gnomes. His mother wrote a letter expressing her desire to see him, but she mentioned nothing about her husband. *He doesn't know*, Calyx decided. He couldn't blame her, though. One day, he knew that he would travel there, or she would visit him in Teversall. Perhaps she would tell Sir Geoffrey eventually. Calyx thought that would be right.

A month after he turned seventeen, a messenger walked into Overton's curios asking for Calyx. "I am he."

"Mr. Overton, Queen Yalena of Brudovel has sent me to ask you to come to the palace. She would like you to cut the diamonds for a special brooch that is to be made for Princess Rhiannon. Will you come?"

Brudovel … the town just beyond the pine forest, where all of the people were under fairies' spells. He had wanted to go there for years. "I will," he replied. "I will need to seek leave from my uncle, however. When would the queen like me to arrive in Brudovel?'

"As soon as possible. The matter is quite urgent. The princess has lost a precious family heirloom and the queen would like a replica made right away. It consists of fifteen rather large diamonds, which she would like you to provide. One is shaped as a teardrop, seven are oblong ovals and seven are circular."

He would have to take a trip to see the gnomes in order to get gems of good quality. He shuddered to think of what they would ask for with a trade that spectacular. He didn't resent it, though. Every trade with the gnomes was a new adventure, and this one, he felt, would be the greatest yet.

"It might take some time to get the diamonds, but I can start on it right away, with my uncle's consent," said Calyx. Before he could ask the messenger to wait while he found his uncle, Tyrone entered the store with an armload of quilted woolen tea cozies. He gave his permission for Calyx to leave as soon as he was ready to do so. He would probably be gone for two weeks or longer.

The messenger told Calyx that he would send out word that the young gem cutter would need lodging, assuring him that the people in Brudovel, though sometimes odd in behavior, were generally quite hospitable. Calyx watched through the front window as the messenger left the store and climbed back into the fresh, regal coach.

Tyrone, who had been to Brudovel a few times, proudly clapped Calyx's back and smiled knowingly.

"Brudovel, you say? My boy, you are in for a treat."

"I'm looking forward to it," Calyx replied with an arch grin.

A bluebird, perched on one of the horse's heads, flew toward the store for a moment, and hung in the air, as if it were taking one last look at Calyx, whose mouth dropped open. In an instant, he understood. He nodded appreciatively and in one elegant swoop, the bird took wing. It merged neatly into the blue sky, flying in the direction that could take it to several other towns within a few hours, one of them being Rimmolan.

# ABOUT THE AUTHOR

When Maia Appleby was in first grade, she received the "Little House on the Prairie" series for Christmas, and she began to read it right away.

By the end of the school year, she had read the whole series at least twice. Donning long brown braids, a sunbonnet and a calico pinafore whenever she could, she wished that she could go back in time and really be Laura Ingalls.

Books do change people. Since then, Maia has loved to read stories that take her to a new place where the characters have different, interesting ways of thinking. She also loves to write them.

Maia lives in Florida with her daughter, a Dog named Dobby, and a bird named Raina. They have a butterfly garden that is so full of passiflora vines that she is pretty sure fairies live in it.

Of course, there is also a garden gnome. His name is Ranzwick.

# BRIGHTER BOOKS

### PUBLISHING HOUSE ™

## Did you love this book?

### Then help us make more like it!

Rate this book on Amazon, GoodReads or your
favorite online book site,
then email us your rating / review to:

star@brighterbooks.com

*and receive an exclusive sneak-peek of one of
our upcoming books!*

Thank you for spreading the word! We are a
small press and need your support to grow!

*Visit www.brighterbooks.com to continue your adventure. . .*

CPSIA information can be obtained at www.ICGtesting.com
Printed in the USA
LVOW052349070812

293349LV00002B/252/P